THE
WORLD'S
FIRST
SALESMAN

THE WORLD'S FIRST SALESMAN

What You Need To Know About Sales Straight From The Caveman Who Invented It

Stuart H. Rosenbaum

Selling Warrior Publishing Co.. San Jose, CA.

Copyright © 2008 by Stuart H. Rosenbaum.

ISBN 978-0-615-57055-6

Library of Congress Registration Number:
TXu 1-576-078

Published by Selling Warrior Publishing Co.
1115 Delmas Ave. # 3. San Jose, CA 95125-1722
www.sellingwarrior.com

Cover and interior desing by A.C. Alongi
www.sigillumpublishers.com

First edition, December 2011.

Printed in the United States of America.

TABLE OF CONTENTS

CHAPTER ONE

JOHNNY'S
REVELATION

CHAPTER ONE

JOHNNY'S REVELATION

Somewhere in Northern California, circa 1999.

As he waited for the light to turn green, Johnny stared at his own tired face in his cracked rearview mirror. He had tried everything, but he knew now that it was time to call it quits. Sales was just not his forte. He had been working for his cousin Lee's electronics firm for nearly a year now, and even though he knew that the firm represented some of the best electronic products available on the market, Johnny wasn't having any success. He simply was not a natural born salesperson.

Johnny thought back to the day he decided to leave behind his profession as a waiter in a prestigious Atlantic City hotel casino restaurant to take this job. Back then, he had felt the promise of something greater in life and dreamt of accomplishing something worthwhile, of being somebody, of riches far beyond what he could earn working in the restaurant. He took the position because Lee, a very successful sales professional himself, had an eye for talent and told Johnny's parents he believed one day Johnny would make a great salesperson. Lee gave Johnny an open invitation to join his firm in California and learn the ropes.

Johnny was twenty-one at the time. He knew he was good looking but that would only take him so far. Although he was a college dropout, he had above-average intelligence and was generally praised by employers for being a hard worker. His waiter job couldn't last forever because he had higher aspirations for himself. He was just a little fuzzy on what those aspirations would be. His cousin's belief in him went a long way and perhaps taking a sales job would open up a whole new world for him. The thought of starting something completely new made him feel nervous and unsure of himself, but he knew he needed a greater challenge in life than waiting tables. He packed up and headed for the west coast to try to make it in sales.

Now a year had passed. Although the charismatic and energetic Lee continued to encourage Johnny with platitudes like, "Hang in their kid" or "Your time will come," Johnny didn't feel right staying on his cousin's payroll. He didn't believe that he had what it would take to be a great salesperson so why should Lee?

Johnny nodded to himself in the mirror as if he and his reflection had finally come to an agreement. He would call his parents in Philadelphia and ask if they might loan

JOHNNY'S REVELATION

him enough money for the airfare home and support him for a while. He needed some time to reassess his life and decide what to do next. Perhaps he would go back to school and finish his degree, or go into law enforcement, or maybe go back to Atlantic City and work in the gaming industry. He didn't know for sure what to do, but he knew, or believed at that moment, he needed to quit sales.

The driver behind Johnny wailed on the horn, and Johnny's car stalled as he fumbled for first gear. Johnny punched his steering wheel with both fists. Although this decision had been weighing on him for some time, it took a rotten day like today to push him over the edge of indecisiveness. Out of five appointments, two of them cancelled and neither buyer bothered to contact Johnny to let him know they wouldn't be able to meet with him. So he drove from his apartment in Redwood City to San Francisco to meet with Mr. Johnson Peabody of Peabody Electronics to present his company's latest assortment of integrated circuits and components. After braving the rush-hour city traffic and stressing over finding a parking spot he could afford, Johnny arrived at the appointment only to have Mr. Peabody's assistant apologize that Mr. Peabody had to cancel for reasons unknown. When Johnny tried to reschedule, she told him not to bother because Mr. Peabody had already placed an order with Johnny's competitor.

Johnny tried not to let the rude rejection get to him as he crossed the Bay Bridge to get to his second appointment, a small custom PC manufacturer in Berkeley. He felt good about this one and had spent some time planning his presentation the night before. He met with the company's component buyer, a stern, fast-talking man in his thirties.

The buyer told Johnny condescendingly, "Look, kid, you've got five minutes so why not just leave the brochures and price lists, and I'll call you if I need anything."

Johnny felt his face burn and his throat constrict. He said, "Give me a chance here. I've put a lot of time into this presentation and if I could just run through it with you…"

The buyer yawned and said, "Sorry kid. I'm real busy. Maybe you can try out your presentation on someone else."

Johnny left, feeling like the world was collapsing on top of him. On his way to his next destination, and since he still wasn't making enough money to afford the expense of a cellular phone, he pulled over to a phone booth to check his messages. Really, his message. As if the face-to-face rejection of the day wasn't enough, it was the credit manager of one of the manufacturers he represented informing him that his only order of the month couldn't be shipped because his customer did not pass credit.

For the rest of the day, Johnny went through the motions of being in sales, but his heart was not in it. He couldn't focus on his presentations or pay attention to what his customers were telling him. He was consumed by feelings of inferiority and a sense that sales was for a certain special kind of person that was not him.

The day ended with the buyer from his last appointment showing him the door and leaving him with the final verdict on his day and what looked like his career: "The truth is I just wouldn't do business with some amateur kid

---

who doesn't know anything about anything. Now scram!"

This, of course, was the final blow.

Johnny parked his car on a side street near downtown Burlingame and contemplated how he would approach his parents about leaving California and coming back home. He got out of the car and walked to a gas station about half a block away, where he knew there was a pay phone. He slowly dialed the number.

His mother answered the phone, "Hello?"

Johnny didn't respond. He couldn't find the right words.

"Hello, who is this?" chimed his mother's voice. "Is anybody there? Who is this?"

Still Johnny didn't respond. Feeling stupid and humiliated, he simply hung up the phone.

Johnny stood in the phone booth with tears in his eyes for a good five minutes. He didn't have the courage to admit to his parents he was a failure. He also knew he didn't have the guts to continue handling the rejection he received in sales. He was torn, not sure what to do or how to handle all these emotions. He thought about his future life but with none of the optimism he had when he decided to move west. Although he was only twenty-two, he felt as though much of his life was over.

His mind raced to find alternatives to the reality that he was a failure. He felt anguished and nervous, even a little light-headed. The world seemed surreal, dream-like, or was it more a nightmare? Pressing in on him from one side was the pain of overcoming rejection and continuing with a sales job that made him feel terrible. On the other side, the shame of quitting and facing the consequences of admitting he was a failure. The pressure was unbearable. Johnny was silently imploding.

Then, like a flash, Johnny had a brief cognition. Sometimes under extreme duress people succumb to the circumstance and buckle under, and sometimes under duress people have an epiphany and rise to a higher state of consciousness with new revelations about life. At that moment, Johnny experienced the latter. Like a vision of divine intervention, Johnny saw how his life would be affected by the decision he made right here and now. The concept was upon him, and then the words flowed from his lips.

Speaking only to himself and not knowing where the words were coming from, Johnny said aloud, "If I can get through this, I can accomplish anything I set my mind to." And then he immediately knew the antithesis to his statement: If he couldn't get through this, then he couldn't accomplish whatever he set his mind to. Even if sales was not his long term career choice, he knew at that moment that he would tough it out and overcome his fears, because conquering those fears was what would determine the success or failure of his life. He would stay in sales and work past his difficulties.

Like Clark Kent walking into a phone booth and coming out as Superman, Johnny emerged from that phone booth a new man. He still had his fears and he knew it. He still had low self-esteem and lacked confidence. He was aware of this. And he still wasn't comfortable with being in sales. What changed was that he now had a mission in life, and that mission was to become more than he had been until that point. He would conquer his fears so he could be whatever he wanted and do what he wanted in life, unlike so many others that are slaves to their own fears.

He walked toward his car with a new vigor in his stride and a plethora of new questions for himself. How would he accomplish this? What could he do differently? How could he take more control of each selling situation? Was there some secret he hadn't learned yet? Was there someone he could talk to? Some books he could read? Would this revelation last? A day? A week? A lifetime?

Uncertainty began to set in again, but this time Johnny was fighting it, pushing it back into his unconscious mind, not validating it. Somehow he realized that all of his negative feelings were not who he really was—this was a new revelation for sure which inspired Johnny to look to the heavens in awe.

Only a few yards from his beat up old Chevy Lumina, a man clad in a fine, tailored Italian suit, with Gucci shoes and Rolex watch exited a bank. He walked backwards as he waved goodbye to someone inside the bank. As Johnny continued to gaze up at the sky, the well styled man in his forties stepped right into Johnny's path. The two collided and Johnny, losing his footing, fell backwards and hit his head on the pavement, knocking him momentarily unconscious. The man knelt at Johnny's side with a concerned look on his face. Others came out of the bank to help.

CHAPTER TWO

THE SALESMAN

CHAPTER TWO

THE SALESMAN

Johnny was unconscious for just a few moments. When he opened his eyes, the man he collided with was still kneeling beside him.

"Sorry," Johnny said. "I feel like such an idiot. I wasn't watching where I was going. I'm really sorry."

With a puzzled look on his face, the man peered into Johnny's eyes and said, "It is I who am sorry young man. I wasn't watching where I was going. But never mind that, we should get you to a hospital and have you checked out. You blanked out for a minute there. We need to make sure you're OK."

Johnny took stock of the man's kind eyes, his attire, and grooming and decided that this was a wealthy man. He appreciated the man's concern but felt stupid and wanted to get out of there. He was embarrassed now with all of the folks that had gathered around to find out what this young man was doing lying on the pavement. The bank manager, a burly man in his fifties with thinning hair and glasses, said he would call an ambulance. Johnny did not feel as though he needed an ambulance.

Johnny stood up, brushed himself off and tried to take control of the situation. He announced, "Thanks for your concern. I think I'm OK, really. There's no need to call an ambulance. I'll be fine."

The wealthy man wouldn't back down. He said with force, "Young man, you took a pretty good blow to the head and my conscience won't allow me to let it go unchecked. The hospital is just a few blocks from here. Come with me. I'll drive you there."

Johnny tried again, "No really, I'm fine, my car's right here." He pointed to his beat up old Chevy Lumina. "I can drive myself, really, thanks."

The man gently placed his hand on Johnny's shoulder. He gave Johnny a stern and somewhat fatherly look. The look told Johnny immediately that this was not a man that you can refuse. "Young man, what's your name?"

"Johnny."

The man said in a soft, but commanding voice, "Johnny, look, you fell and hurt your head. I can't let you take the chance of driving right now. You're coming with me to the hospital to get checked out. Do you understand?"

"Yessir."

"Good. My car's just across the street."

They crossed the street and approached the man's car, which instantly affirmed Johnny's suspicions that this

_____

was a rich man. The car was a new, black Mercedes S550 with leather interior and all the trimmings. Johnny had never been in such an expensive automobile before.

He got in the passenger seat and said, "Nice car!"

"Thanks," the man said. "I just bought it a month ago. Really handles well. Very comfortable. By the way, Johnny, my name is Chance. Chance McNulty."

"Thanks for taking me Mr. McNulty. I appreciate it. It isn't everyday that a stranger shows this kind of concern for someone."

"Not a problem, Johnny. Call me Chance."

"OK, Chance. This car, the payments must be astronomical," Johnny exclaimed.

"No payments. I paid cash."

"Wow. You must be rich."

"I do OK, Johnny. I've been lucky to make a good living in my business. I picked the right career," Chance responded.

"What do you do?" asked Johnny.

"I'm in sales," Chance replied.

"Wow. Really? Wow. I'm in sales, too. Electronics. I obviously haven't done as well as you have. I'm impressed. You bought this car with your sales income?"

"Sure. Why not? Sales, is the greatest profession there is. It's given me an incredible lifestyle. Nice home, vacation home, forty-foot sailing schooner, investments, and a happy misses at home with two kids in college. If I had to do it all again, I wouldn't change anything. I love sales. I love my customers, business associates, the friends

I've made. I guess you can say I've been blessed," Chance explained.

"That sounds amazing," Johnny responded. "I wish I felt the same way about sales as you do."

"What do you mean by that Johnny?" Chance asked.

"Well, I've been trying, but I guess I'm just not a natural born salesperson. I mean, I haven't really made any money at it. It's tough. Maybe it's what I'm selling, I don't know. What do you sell?"

"Insurance. Life Insurance."

"Huh?" Johnny responded, "I thought that was the toughest thing there is to sell. I mean, don't you have to remind people that they're going to die and stuff in order to get them to buy it?"

Chance laughed. He remembered his first year in sales and thinking about how difficult it would be. He answered, "You know Johnny, sales isn't really about what you sell, but how you practice the art of selling and how you treat your customers. See, for example, in the life insurance business it's not about reminding people that they're going to die. It's about the quality of life that the product can bring them. I mean, if you're a father and a husband, you care about your family and you want to provide them with everything they need in the event something unfortunate happens. Once you know that you've secured your family's future, you can enjoy your own life with less worry."

"Well put. I can see why you're a great salesperson," Johnny stated.

Sensing that Johnny was probably a young man at

THE SALESMAN

the crossroads in life with some self-doubts and not a lot of confidence and realizing that he himself had experienced this very same challenge earlier in life, Chance decided he would help young Johnny. Perhaps he could offer some timely advice that, if properly taken and applied, could transform Johnny's life for the better.

Chance started, "You know Johnny, I wasn't born this way. Being good in sales wasn't a gift. You hear people say that a salesperson is someone with the 'gift of gab,' but it's really not true. When I was about your age, you're probably, what? About twenty-four, twenty-five?"

Johnny answered, "Twenty-two actually."

"...Twenty-two. OK, well I was twenty-four when I got into sales. Just married, already had a kid on the way, graduated college with a bachelor's degree. You know, you can't do much with a bachelor's degree— thought I would go to grad school, but never made it. Anyhow, that's when I got into insurance sales. The first year was a real struggle—the rejection, the objections people had that I couldn't handle, the nervousness. No one's born a salesperson. You have to learn it. It's a profession like any other profession. You have to learn, practice, study, and perfect your skills. You even have to go back to school from time to time."

"School?" Johnny asked.

"Well, yeah. Sales school. I mean there are always new products and those are easy to learn about. What I mean is going back to hone your skills, you know, prospecting, presenting, handling objections, closing."

Johnny had a dumb look on his face. Chance picked

this up and immediately understood the situation.

Chance said to Johnny, "So, you've never had any formal education in sales? No sales training? Do you know what the sales cycle is?"

"Oh, yes," Johnny responded. "The sales cycle. I know that's like when the manufacturers make certain products that are available for a certain period, and we have to sell them. And at different times of the year, sales are higher than at other times and...."

Chance cut him off, laughing gently. "No, no, no. There's an actual cycle in sales. A step-by-step process you have to follow if you want to be successful at closing sales. It's like the universal game plan of sales, without which we'd all be lost."

"There is? Where do I get it?" Johnny asked eagerly.

Just then, Chance turned his car into the parking lot of St. Mary's Hospital. "Let's get you checked out and then I can tell you about the sales cycle."

The two men walked into the emergency room and met the nurse on duty. The nurse asked some questions, gave Johnny some papers to complete, and as is uncharacteristic in a hospital emergency room, almost immediately escorted Johnny back to one of the available examination rooms. Chance let Johnny know he'd wait for him in the waiting room. Chance then pulled out his cell phone and called his wife to explain what happened and that he would be home late. They agreed she wouldn't worry about Chance's dinner; perhaps he'd grab a bite with the young man, before heading home.

CHAPTER THREE

THE PROFESSION OF SALES

THE PROFESSION OF SALES

C hance waited the hour it took for the emergency staff to examine Johnny. When Johnny returned to the lobby he was with a small Indian Doctor, Dr. Jawani. The doctor explained to Chance that Johnny had a small bruise and suffered a mild concussion. It wasn't really anything to worry about. Chance was relieved to hear the news and he and Johnny returned to his car. Chance checked his watch. It was only 6:30 pm.

By now, Johnny was anxious to learn more from the older man, and so he was elated when Chance offered to buy him dinner and share some advice with him. It occurred to Johnny that none of this would be happening now if he hadn't spent exactly five minutes in that phone booth on this day at that time and had the epiphany that he'd had. A small miracle seemed to be unfolding in his life. He recalled something he once read or heard from some motivational speaker—that once you decided to accomplish something,

"Heaven and earth will then move in mysterious ways to help you accomplish the goal."

Chance picked a small coffee shop at a commuter railway station that he knew had good food and was quiet, a good place for conversation. Once inside, they received menus and promptly ordered. Then Chance settled in to give Johnny some much-needed advice to help him develop the determination and skills to succeed.

Chance began, "Well, the first bit of advice I can give you about sales, I've already touched on. Unbeknownst to many, sales is truly a profession that has been crafted and perfected over thousands of years, just like medicine, law, and accounting. Once you recognize that sales is a profession, then you have to decide to become a professional. That means all of the study and practice that go along with being expert in any field. You see, too often salespeople treat sales like a job they do because they have nothing else to do.

"Once you've decided to be a professional, you must lay out a path of learning. This means reading and listening to tapes. It means you need to practice closing techniques, objection-handling techniques, prospecting techniques, and you need to become an expert on your products. One of my mentors, a world-renowned sales trainer, used to tell me "As a professional, you must always lead the client to the decision you've already made for them."

Johnny blurted, "But that doesn't sound honest."

"Not so, my young grasshopper," Chance replied with a fatherly Chinese accent. "This is perhaps the greatest service you can perform for your clients. You see, you have to know their needs and desires first, but then you guide them to the proper solution. People are sometimes nervous about spending money. They grow up on fear-based advice from their parents and friends like, 'Don't act too hastily' or 'Sleep on it' or 'Beware of fast talking salesmen,' so they end up too intimidated to make a decision that's good for them—even when it's the right decision. You see, I would never sell a client a $100,000 life policy if I knew that their family would need $250,000. I would be performing a disservice to my client, and his or her family. When you fully understand their needs, you have a duty and an obligation to ensure that they make the right decision."

Johnny asked, "Well, what if they needed a $250,000 policy, but you could sell them a million dollar policy? Wouldn't you do that to get a bigger commission?"

Chance smiled. He was hoping for this question. "Never. I would never oversell the client deliberately just for a larger commission. I know in my heart that if I fulfill my client's needs, and that is my only goal, I will surely be rewarded. The reward is, first, a satisfied client, and, second, a commission, and last, a life-long relationship—maybe even a good friend—that will refer me clients every time he hears of someone that needs life insurance. It's not about the money. If you focus on the money, you won't earn much. If you focus on the client's needs, you'll earn all the money you can count and a lifetime of self-respect and dignity. You should never feel bad about making a sale and that means you only provide what the client truly needs."

Johnny brightened up. "I never knew that. I mean,

I never even thought of it. My boss says just to sell what's in stock. I never really considered what the client wanted over what I was supposed to sell!"

"Good. You're catching on. So now you know. Always remember to lead the client to the decision that you know is right for them.

"The next thing to know about sales is that your knowledge of people and people skills are far more important than your product knowledge."

"But if I don't have the product knowledge, then how will I know what to sell them?" Johnny asked.

"Don't misunderstand. You must know your products and be an expert at them. You have to know perfectly well which products are suitable for which clients. But, even more importantly, if you are to guide people towards making important decisions, you must understand people. What are their likes, dislikes, fears, tendencies, defense mechanisms, tells."

"What's a tell?"

"Tell is a term usually used in poker, but really a tell is a sign that someone does unconsciously, but that tells you something about what they're thinking or how they're feeling. For example, if I cross my arms like this and back away from the table, what does that tell you?"

"Well, you look bored. Maybe you're not interested, I guess?"

"Precisely. Now, if I move forward, closer to you and look intently like this, what does that tell you?"

Johnny responded while nodding up and down with

understanding, "I got it. So now you're interested. Your body language shows me. OK. I got it."

"Good. So that's a tell. Basically, telltale gestures, posture, comments and so on that let you know how your presentation is going over with your client. You want to understand their fears, so you can disarm them. Fear, my friend, is a salesperson's true enemy. Their fear and yours. If you show fear, they'll sense it and they'll feel it themselves. It could be said that in order to close a sale, you need to bring the client up from a state of fear to a state of enlightenment.

Chance continued, "So you see, the professional truly learns the art of understanding people. They also have to learn the art of communication. When to listen, when to talk, when to acknowledge the customer and let them know you heard them, and when to check to see if they understand you. If you attempt to communicate, but they don't understand, then your communication is not really reaching them, is it?"

"No, I guess not."

Just then, their food arrived. Both took a fork full, and Chance continued between chews of his chicken Caesar salad.

"So, let me recap where we are so far," said Chance, "First, the decision to be a professional, next is the studying part, then learning about and understanding people and, of course, mastering the skills of communication. You got it so far?"

"Yes. Professionalism, Study, People, Communication. I got it!"

"Good," Chance paused to take a sip of his iced tea, "Next is dedication to hard work. This one escapes many of my less successful colleagues. I like to say that I personally take a blue-collar approach to a white-collar profession. What I mean by that statement is that I roll up my sleeves and get to work. I put in the time—no monkey business. I don't spend any time during the day dawdling around. I go from one call to the next, one prospect to another, and when I don't have a prospect to talk with immediately, I prospect for more."

"Except for when you have to go to the bank to deposit your paychecks, like you were doing this afternoon," joked Johnny.

"Actually, the bank manager is my client. I was their taking an application for an increase in his coverage."

"Oh," Johnny said, feeling stupid.

"You see, Johnny, sales is like any other business where the more you put in, the more you get out of it. For example, take Barry Bonds. He takes his conditioning seriously. He probably takes more batting practice than anyone on his team. The more he swings, the more he hones his skill and timing. So you see in sales, the more prospects you talk to or get in front of, the more opportunities you have to do two very important things."

"What are they?"

"Close a sale…"

"Of course," Johnny exclaimed.

"….And sharpen your skills. It's true that sales is a numbers game. Even a very bad salesperson will get business if they talk to enough prospects. All the sales training, product knowledge, people knowledge and communication skills one can muster won't amount to anything if you don't do the numbers. Keep statistics. How many people you contact, number of appointments made, number of presentations made, sales, and your income. You see, if you don't keep stats religiously, you'll never know for sure how you got the results that you got. For example, let's say I've made more sales calls and appointments in one week than I ever have in the past. Suppose for some reason however my sales are down and my income is low. I've been doing the numbers, so I know that something else is wrong and needs to be fixed, understand?"

"Yeah, I get it. You did the numbers, but sales are low. That means what you have to fix has something to do with your technique or presentation."

"Now you're getting it kid! I'm proud of you. You're catching on."

"So then what do you do?" Johnny asked, with an eager look on his face.

"You fix it! You find out what's wrong and you fix it!" responded Chance.

"How?"

"Well, I'll tell you about the sales cycle, and then you'll understand. But before I do, I want you to understand this thing about the numbers. Remember, the greatest closer in the world is nothing, if he doesn't have any prospects. You have to make the calls, generate tons of new prospects all the time—even when you think you have enough—you never do. If your numbers are up and sales are down, then it's something in your technique, communication, or presentation. If the technique is sound and communication good but you aren't making enough sales, you just have to up the numbers! And, like the baseball analogy I gave you, with properly applied technique, the more prospects you speak with the faster you hone your sales skills. Even Barry Bonds has the occasional slump. So what does he do? He finds out what's wrong with his swing or timing and figures out how to correct it. Then he practices it, taking extra batting practice to perfect it. Often, he uses a coach to help him identify what's wrong."

"OK, but where do you get a coach in sales?" Johnny asked.

Chance replied, "That's simple. That's what the sales manager is for. However, if the sales manager doesn't practice the same skills and techniques then they'll be useless. So that's when you attend sales trainings, listen to tapes, and team up with other professionals so you can coach each other."

"Sounds fun! But I don't have any techniques. I mean, I have no idea what's wrong or right when it comes to sales," Johnny said with exasperation in his voice.

"Johnny, years ago, when I was twenty-five, about a year after I got into sales, I thought I would quit the profession. I thought it wasn't for me. It was too hard. Too much rejection. I thought about going back to school to get my masters degree. I figured I could go to school in the daytime and tend bar at night to feed the family. I didn't

THE PROFESSION OF SALES

know exactly how it would work out. I just knew sales wasn't for me."

As Chance was speaking, Johnny clung to his every word. He couldn't believe what he was hearing. It had to be a dream. This wonderful man accidentally comes into his life to share his experience of twenty years earlier—the exact same experience that Johnny was having at present.

Johnny asked, "Well what made you stay in sales?"

"I got lucky. I was at the right place at the right time. It happened on my twenty-fifth birthday actually. I was at a party for me. A surprise party. About 50 of my friends and relatives were there. At first I was elated. But later on in the evening, I found myself sitting outside of my parents' house on the patio by myself, feeling dejected. Eventually my father came looking for me. He asked what was wrong, so I told him how it was going in the insurance business and that I was thinking of quitting. He asked me if at any point I ever felt excited about getting into sales. I told him yes. Then he told me to take the afternoon off the next day and come by his office, that he had something to share with me. I agreed. The rest is history."

"What? Come on. What happened then?" Johnny begged.

Chance laughed in a sinister tone. "He told me The Story of Ug and his Revolutionary Invention."

"Huh?" Johnny looked bewildered.

"You know: The Story of Ug and his Revolutionary Invention!" Chance said, knowingly toying with the younger man, trying to build up the suspense.

"What the…. Who is….huh?

Chance laughed, "I'm just having some fun with you kid."

"You mean you just made that up, this Ug character?"

"Heavens no. He's real… I mean, the story. But if I start now, I might not finish it until late. We could be here until midnight," Chance said, checking his watch.

Johnny, desperate for information, "Please tell me. I'll buy dinner. I'll buy desert. Tell it to me. Please."

Chance planned to tell him anyway. It had been years since his father related this magical tale to him and the knowledge it imparted had literally changed Chance's life. His sales career had started to skyrocket almost immediately from that point. But Chance, older now and having grown wiser through the years, knew well that for the information to have an impact, the student had to be eager to receive it. The student's mind had to be in a heightened state of awareness. Before Chance began, he checked the closing time of the restaurant. He didn't want to be interrupted. Finding that the diner closed at 1:00 am, he ordered coffee for both of them and continued Johnny's education.

"You see, Johnny, my father was a very successful salesman himself. He traveled the world working for IBM, selling mainframe systems to large corporations. I had the great benefit of growing up in a family that could give me anything I wanted. Not that they did, however, but they could. My father retired from IBM about twelve years ago, a very wealthy man. He has a library at the house full of sales awards. The amazing thing is that his father, my grandfather, was also a great salesman. When my father saw the anguish on my face, my despair over my inability to be effective in sales, he took me under his wing and taught me some of the things I've just shared with you."

"But you got into sales a year earlier, why didn't he help you when you first started?"

"You know, I asked him the same question."

"What did he say?" asked Johnny.

"He told me that the best time to learn a valuable lesson is when you're ready to receive the information. When I first got into sales, my confidence was high and I thought I could conquer the world. I had to get kicked around a bit, to suffer defeat, and to feel beaten in order to get to a state where I would crave the information."

"Kind of the way I feel right now," Johnny mumbled.

Chance smiled. From the first few moments that they spoke in Chance's car, he knew that Johnny would feel this way. Chance had decided early on that he would share this information with Johnny because he saw that hungry look in the young man's eyes, and he liked Johnny. He also remembered that he made a solemn vow to his father that, when the time was right, he would share the wisdom and the magical story and help enrich someone else's career in sales and their life. In order for the story to live, it had to be shared from one person to another. As far as anyone knew, the story hadn't been written down anywhere.

Chance forewarned Johnny, "Now, Johnny, the story I'm about to tell you has been passed down through the ages, and only the very worthy have benefited from its content.

THE WORLD'S
FIRST SALESMAN

When you were a little boy I'm sure you heard some fairy tales, right?"

"Yes."

"Okay, because the way I'm going to tell you this story sounds like a fairy tale, so don't get funny about it. It's just the way I heard it and my father and his father before him. OK?"

"OK!" Johnny didn't care if the story was in rhymed couplets. He just wanted Chance to hurry up and tell it!

CHAPTER FOUR

UG AND THE REVOLUTIONARY INVENTION

CHAPTER FOUR

UG AND THE REVOLUTIONARY INVENTION

Chance began his story.

Long, long ago, somewhere on Earth, lived a caveman whose name was Ug. Ug was a family man. He lived with his cave wife and three cave kids. They lived happily and peacefully with their neighbors at the base of the foothills on the edge of a great valley. They called it the Valley of the Sun because the sun was often blocked out by the hills, but the further one moved into the valley, the more sun one could see. But words were kind of experimental back then so their community was just starting out in the business of naming things. Ug himself was responsible for most of the words and names they were using.

Ug was an industrious guy, an inventor of sorts. One of his inventions was a container made of goatskin that enabled him and his neighbors to carry water from the abundantly flowing valley streams back to the cave and store the water. Ug was considered by his neighbors to be a benevolent guy, a quiet leader.

In the Valley of the Sun, there was no government, as government hadn't really been invented yet. However, the neighbors did have an understanding that each individual cave family was entitled to their own belongings and so each respected the other's property.

Ug's next-door neighbor, or I should say next-cave neighbor, was a big hulk of a guy, who towered nearly a full foot over Ug. His name was Erf. Ug and Erf were the best of friends. They hunted together, swam together, gathered firewood together, did tree swinging together, worked together, and played games together. When one had to venture out into the valley alone, the other would watch over his friend's family. Erf always considered his friend Ug to be somewhat of a genius, a cave dwelling sort of DaVinci.

One day, food stocks were getting low and Ug and Erf decided it was time to venture deep into the valley to hunt. Many of their neighbors joined them, for it was time for all families to stock up on fresh meat and hides for the coming weeks ahead. In all there were nine of them—Ug, Erf, Ug's brother Mug, Krat, Mup, Pung, Wup, Ruh, and Gork. In those days, Ug and his friends had only one option for traveling and that was on foot. The hunters knew they were in for a long and grueling journey.

At dawn, wives and children lined up to bid their husbands and fathers a safe trip. The men all hoped their women and children would be safe, and each left the oldest

---

boy in charge of protecting the family. The men set off on their journey.

Their route would take them through the Thick Forest, over the Hills of Lug, and across the Stream of Ghosts. By modern standards, this would be about a fifteen-minute drive on the freeway, but for Ug and his companions, it was like traveling worlds away. It would take four moons—or as we know it, four days—to complete the whole journey, the longest trip of the year.

During the autumn and winter months in the Valley of the Sun, the game would head to the warmer climate and sun deeper in the valley. The men needed to kill the game that would be eaten on the trip and on the trip home. However, in order to stock food for their families to eat over the course of the next season, they would have to bring back much of the game alive.

This always presented a problem of transportation. The animals were wild and wouldn't simply walk back home with the men. Therefore, upon catching the game, they would tie them up and drag them back home, sliding them on hides obtained from earlier kills. The process took four moons because the hunters needed a full day's journey to reach the part of the valley where they would find game, another day to complete their hunting, and two full days to return with the catch. The return trip was burdensome and slow.

As the men trekked out across the valley, they occupied themselves by making up new words, experimenting with language and storytelling in their new cave tongue.

THE WORLD'S
FIRST SALESMAN

They also sang songs, which were a mish mash of humming and grunting, and they played a game of throwing rocks at various targets. By mid-day the travelers ventured into the Thick Forest. The forest provided some much needed shade from the scorching afternoon sun. Yet, some of the men were superstitious and afraid of the dense, dark forest. Ug encouraged them to stick together in case they encountered any ghosts or other harmful beings that they believed resided in the forest and in the stream farther down the valley.

Erf, Mup, and Krat were particularly afraid of the forest and wanted to hurry through without stopping to rest. Ug referred to them as a bunch of "Waaas"—cave-speak for "babies." The Waas were overruled and the men stopped and made a lunch camp at the base of a big rock that leaned against a giant redwood tree. Mug, Ug's younger brother and Erf's neighbor to the north, began the long process of smacking flint stones together to start the fire. Mup, Krat, and Pung gathered dried leaves and kindling wood for the fire.

Meanwhile, Erf, who was the largest of the nine men, thundered over to a nearby tree to relieve himself. Suddenly he heard something rustling in the leaves. He stopped what he was doing and listened intently as he felt the familiar prickle of fear spread across the back of his neck. Grabbing a stick, he swooshed the leaves aside. Something jumped out at him, but it happened too fast to see what it was. Whatever it was it scared the daylights out of him. He ran towards the others with his stick pointing over his shoulder, yelling, "Ahhh! Ahhh!" which is cave speak for

UG AND THE REVOLUTIONARY INVENTION

"Ahhh! Ahhh!"—undoubtedly the origin of the word.

Not looking where he was going, Erf ran straight through the fire that Mug had started and caught the hair of his foot on fire. He proceeded to hop in circles around the camp, holding his burning foot and screaming, "Ahhh, Ahhh!" The others could not believe his lunacy and their good luck at witnessing such a hilarious event. Krat was laughing so hard he was lying face down, banging both his hands and feet on the ground.

Ug laughed but was a little more empathetic. Realizing they might not have enough water to waste on Erf's stupidity, Ug threw a hide on the foot and smothered the fire. Throughout lunch, the others kept pointing at Erf's foot and laughing, making jokes. Luckily, Erf only singed the hair and did not badly burn the skin, so he was able to continue the journey.

CHAPTER FIVE

THE HUNT

CHAPTER FIVE

THE HUNT

The cave dwellers ate their lunch, packed their supplies, and continued on their journey. By late afternoon, they exited the east side of the forest. The Hills of Lug were just ahead, about a forty-minute journey from the forest. The Hills of Lug were no where near as steep or as large as the foothills above the cave dwellers' homes, and it wasn't much of a task to cross them on the way to the hunt. However, the return trip over the hills would be grueling because they had to "lug" the game. This made even the smallest hills challenging. The men made the journey over the hills in two hours and were approaching the Stream of Ghosts as the sun was beginning to set far to the west towards the base of the foothills where they began their journey. They would get to the western edge of the stream and make camp for the night. In the morning, they would cross the stream into what they referred to this time of year as the Valley of Meat because game was so abundant there.

The day began with the sounds of whistling birds splashing in the nearby stream, diving for fish. Ug was the first to rise. He stood up, stretched, and kicked his brother Mug. Eventually the men were all awake and busy rubbing the sleep from their eyes. They shared a large side of gazelle meat for a tasty and hearty breakfast and then organized themselves for the trek across the stream. They called it the Stream of Ghosts because at night it was common to hear a ghostlike "whooo, whooo," echoing through the valley.

Once they crossed the stream, they were rewarded by the stunning view out over a vast expanse of the Valley of the Sun filled with a caveman's delight—fresh meat! Their first task was to hunt and kill enough game for the next few days and nights. They estimated that they would need three gazelles or one gazelle and one wildebeest. Erf and Mug sharpened their spears while Pung, Krat, and Mup strategized the group's best positioning to begin the chase. They decided that three men would scare the game to run in the direction of the other six men who would be waiting with spears. Once they had killed enough for their stay, they would begin the more difficult task of trapping live game to be taken home for fresh meat later.

Pung, Krat, and Mup took their positions. Erf, Mug, Wup, Ruh, Gork, and Ug stood ready by the side of the stream. When they were all set, Ug gave the signal. Pung, Krat, and Mup ran directly toward a pack of gazelles hollering and whooping until the gazelles made a break towards the stream. Ug was the first to strike, and one gazelle

___

hit the ground instantly. Erf, the biggest, but not exactly the most coordinated of the group, simply stepped out from behind the tree and held out his spear as the gazelles neared. Luck was with him and one gazelle ran right into it. Two down, one to go. Gork, who was a keen shot with a spear, stepped forward next and nailed one from thirty feet. The men cheered. With the first task completed, they were assured they had enough to eat while they finished their hunt.

After a long lunch break, Ug gathered the men together to plan their next steps. Each man had enough strength to drag about three bound critters home to their families. After much deliberation, the men agreed on a plan, which was really just the reverse of the first plan. This time six men would chase the animals into the stream to slow them down, Then, the three largest men, Erf, Gork, and Krat would tackle one each and hold them down as the others bound their feet. They would have to perform this exercise an exhausting nine times in order to obtain enough meat to take home.

The operation was moving along successfully. During the remainder of the first day, they captured twelve animals. By lunchtime the next day, they had a total of twenty-four. Only one more pursuit to go. The six chasers surrounded a group of grazing gazelles, each hoping that this was it and they could return home.

The chase began. Two gazelles immediately tried to make their way across the stream. Gork grabbed the first one and tackled it hard into the water, while Ug and Mug jumped into the stream to bind it. Next, Krat grabbed a big one and Mup and Ruh were immediately there to help. Only one more to go. Pung got behind a gazelle and chased it towards the water, but when it got close to the bank it encountered Erf and instinctively knew it would be trapped. The gazelle veered away before actually entering the stream. Not sticking with the plan, Erf decided to chase the gazelle. It might have worked except the clumsy Erf stepped on a large jagged rock, causing a deep wound in the soul of his foot with the singed hair.

"Ahhh!!!! Ahhh!!!" yelled Erf. His foot was oozing blood. Ug and the other men came to his aid and helped him into the water to wash his foot.

After cleaning the wound as best he could, Ug wrapped his friend's foot in one of the hides brought from home to be used to slide their game back to their caves. It looked serious and Ug was fairly sure that Erf could not walk, let alone drag his load. This was terrible news for the group because Erf weighed nearly three hundred pounds. It would take two of the others to drag him home using at least two more of the hides. This meant that there would be only six men to carry the game, and they were short three hides to transport the game.

Ug called the others over to discuss the issue. He needed a bright idea, but none of the men had one to offer. Soon night fell on their encampment. Preoccupied, Ug wandered away from the group and walked along the bank of the stream in the bright moonlight. Mug saw his older brother go and joined him, bringing along a joint of delicious gazelle meat.

CHAPTER FIVE
THE HUNT

The two brothers strolled in silence about two hundred yards from the encampment. Mug finished his dinner and threw the bone into the stream. To keep himself occupied, Mug kicked any rocks or twigs he found in his path. When they came to a large rounded tree limb, Mug ran over to it and kicked it heartily. The limb began to roll slowly, picked up speed, and then launched off the edge of the bank and splashed into the stream below. Ug watched this action indifferently. After progressing another fifty feet or so, a light went on in Ug's head and he turned to look back at where the limb had been. That rolling tree limb might just be the answer! Perhaps the cavemen could utilize this phenomenon to help transport their game and Erf back to their cave village.

Ug found two more tree limbs and placed another longer tree limb across the first two. He demonstrated to Mug how the tree limbs could be used.

"Genius," thought Mug, proud that he had contributed to solving the problem. The two ran back to the encampment and told the others. They decided to build a larger contraption in the morning after a good night's rest.

And thus the first wheel was invented!

CHAPTER SIX

THE WHEEL

CHAPTER SIX

THE WHEEL

"Wow, so that's how the wheel was invented," Johnny exclaimed. "Interesting story so far, but I don't get what this has to do with sales?"

"Oh, you will soon enough," replied Chance. "You see that's the rest of the story. Let's order some dessert and I'll finish it.

"Great," proclaimed Johnny.

The next day the cavemen managed to break off two very thick rounded tree limbs and several long sturdy ones. They tied some of the hides to the long and sturdy ones to create a floor that would keep the game from falling off. They then used more hides to attach the floor to the rounded tree limbs they used for wheels. Ug also got the idea to cut some grooves in the wheels where the hides would bind the carriage portion. They then tied the remaining hides to the front of the cart and used these to pull it. Wouldn't you know it, their crude invention actually worked! They were truly elated.

The men piled most of the game on top of this enormous cart and then Erf climbed on the back. It was extremely heavy, and they determined that it would take four men to pull the contraption. The other four men had to slide the remaining game the way they always did it.

They set out, thrilled with the success of their new invention. Although it fell apart three times on the way, each time they were able to successfully repair it and get on their way without too much delay.

When they arrived at the cave village right on schedule at the end of the fourth day, all of the cave wives, children, elders, and remaining cave men came to see this new invention. At first there was just an awed silence, and then the cave people erupted into cheers for Ug and the men. A celebratory feast was planned.

Ug felt an enormous sense of accomplishment, thinking he may have created the most important invention of cave mankind. He began to envision how this new invention could reshape the world they lived in. He was sure he'd be hailed a hero in cave villages everywhere if he could bring this new technology to others like him. He decided that this would be his mission for the rest of his days.

Almost immediately, fear set in and diluted his excitement. If this was to be his mission in life, how would he have time to hunt and feed his family? This concern tormented him and he pondered it for days. Finally, he had an idea. He and Mug and the newly healed Erf could go to other villages and trade wheels for game. "Wow, what a concept!" he thought. They would take a load of wheels, unload them at the other villages, and reload his cart with food. By doing this they could skip the regular hunting trip and spend that time with their families. This was the first spark for another one of Ug's great inventions, "Commerce"!

Ug took the next few months to perfect the design of the wheel. His idea was to cut sections of large tree limbs into round discs and then cut holes in the middle. This way another limb could fit crossways through the holes of two wheels and even more limbs and animal skins could be bound to these crossway limbs, making a more stable cart. He took a stick and drew out his design in the dirt. He called his new business partners, Erf and Mug and consulted their opinions. They agreed it was a much superior model.

"Only one problem," Mug said. "How do we cut these sections of tree limbs into discs?"

This was a problem, indeed. Ug thought about it for days. One day, as he and Erf were barbequing up a side of gazelle meat, he asked Erf how his foot was. Erf told him it was much better and that he would be careful not to step on any sharp rocks again. Just then another light went on inside the head of the now great inventor Ug. He grabbed his stick and quickly ran to his then modern-day drafting table, the dirt pile outside his cave. He drew up a design for a device that tied a large sharp rock to a strong stick. A device that could be used for chopping and cutting. And, thus, Ug invented the axe!

Ug the genius inventor and now CEO of Ug

Enterprises sent his two junior partners Erf and Mug out to scour the village to find the sharpest flat rocks they could. They returned half a day later with several rocks that seemed to fit Ug's needs. Ug fastened the most favorable rock with animal skin to a strong stick. He then wet the skin and let it dry in the sun. The next day, the binding was tight enough to give the new axe a try—and to his great surprise and elation, AHA!!! It worked. Now the three entrepreneurs could get to the task of creating a better cart. They spent the next several weeks manufacturing axes and wheels and axles and then assembling them into carts. Then they prepared for their first test—their first road show to the nearby cave village known as Grump.

CHAPTER SEVEN

THE TRIP TO GRUMP

CHAPTER SEVEN

THE TRIP TO GRUMP

U g, Erf, Mug, and their newest employee, Krat, had the carts all loaded and ready for their two-day journey to the Village of Grump. All the wives and kids were there to wish them well and see them off. The four men were excited to hit the road. They were proud pioneers. Another concept began to develop in their minds when Ug told them of his vision of how they would trade goods for food and other goods. This concept was the concept of wealth. Now back then there wasn't yet much to spend any newly acquired wealth on, but they began to envision larger caves with new amenities such as bigger water vessels and places to park their newly invented carts. The possibilities seemed endless.

The two-day trip to Grump was tiring and uneventful. When they arrived at the outskirts of Grump, they encountered a little boy. Krat smiled at the boy, who immediately ran to towards the village, yelling for anyone who would listen. Ug and his men pressed on. By the time they arrived at the center of the village, several villagers had gathered to see the new men from a far-away land and their new contraptions.

One very old cave man with white hair and a long beard spoke first. He appeared to be their leader. But neither Ug nor any of the others could understand what he was saying. The man approached Ug. He held out his hand and pointed towards Ug. In Ug's village the act of pointing at someone was considered an act of disrespect so Ug took immediate offense. What Ug didn't know was that in the Village of Grump, the act of pointing was a form of greeting. Ug began to yell at the man. Not understanding a word that Ug was saying, the man, began to yell back at him. The villagers became agitated and the situation escalated.

Ug and the old man shouted at each other in their own languages and the villagers and Ug's men did the same. A few villagers even picked up rocks and threw them at Erf, Mug, and Krat. Before too long there was a complete onslaught of shouts and rocks all targeting the new entrepreneurs.

A terrible sense of regret and a sense of failure flooded over Ug. This entire idea was just a huge waste of time. But before he could wallow in his own negative attitude, Ug decided he better act quickly for the safety of his own men. He ran for the carts, hoping they'd get the idea. The men were by his side in an instant. With the villagers' angry shouts escorting them out, Ug and his men scurried out of

Grump and made their way for home.

The men felt more than a little dejected. They all agreed that their mission was obviously futile and they should hang up their axes and go back to life as normal in their own village. They didn't want to admit their own failure. What would their wives, children and the elders of the village think of them now? They decided to make up a story, an excuse—Yes! They would blame their failure on the people of Grump.

Together they crafted a tale that depicted the people of Grump as mean and nasty people that nobody could get along with. From the old man with the white beard to the youngest child in the village, they were all long-faced and cruel. Ug decided on a new word to describe them, "Grumpy!!" He referred to their leader with the white hair and beard as the "Grumpy Old Man!"

They arrived back to their village after sundown on the fourth day of their trip. The last two days were the longest days of their lives. They quietly entered their caves, greeted their wives and children, and agreed they would share their story with the whole village the next morning.

The next morning, all of the villagers, men, women, children, and elders gathered around in a large circle to hear the story of their brave pioneers' trip to far-away Grump. Ug retold the story that the four men had agreed to share with the others. When he got to the part about the old man pointing and the argument that ensued, the oldest living elder in the village raised his eyebrows in heightened under-standing. Ug took one hour to tell the story. The villagers were disappointed. Some even suggested declaring war on Grump. Ug quickly dismissed that idea saying that war never resolved anything.

The crowd quietly dispersed. Al, the elder, approached Ug. He put a hand on the younger man's shoulder and told him he needed to speak with him in his cave. This is the story he told the young inventor.

Many, many moons ago when Al was a young man, he and his father and some of the other villagers went on a hunt. Back in those days, there was less game and it moved around more. In order to catch some, you had to figure out where the game went according to the season. Al and his men went on a two-day trek that eventually landed them in the Village of Grump. These men were in need of food and a place to rest. The villagers of Grump welcomed them. They gave the men food, water, and a place to rest. When the men were feeling better, the villagers pointed them in the direction of a large flock of gazelles fresh for the killing.

During their stay in Grump, Al learned a thing or two about Grump customs. One of these customs was their method of greeting new people, which was to point at them. Al told Ug that at first he was surprised because in his own village he knew that pointing was a disrespectful act. But in Grump, pointing was simply a friendly greeting method.

Ug stayed quiet for some time. He was embarrassed that he had told the other villagers so many bad things about the people of Grump, including his new word for them, "grumpy." Al told Ug he understood Ug's dilemma and why he felt he had to tell such a story. But the truth was that the people of Grump are really caring people. Because Ug misunderstood them, he caused a difficult situation for himself and his men. Al let Ug know that he wouldn't share this story with anyone else and that he knew Ug needed some time to work things out for himself.

Ug wondered what he could have done differently. Taking himself and three other men on a four-day trek and having no results was costly indeed for Ug's new enterprise. Then, like a lightening bolt strikes an electrical tower in modern times, it hit him. What Ug needed to do was to Properly Greet People.

If he knew the proper greeting for the people of Grump, he might have been successful in his venture to trade wheels for food. "That's it!" thought Ug. "You have to have a Proper Greeting in order to be successful." Ug found new hope with this revelation. He immediately told Al, who smiled and patted Ug on the back.

Ug decided he would share his newest revelation with Erf, Krat, and Mug. He quickly called a meeting. Ug started out by telling them that the business was back on because he had figured out what they could have done differently to achieve success. This was not what the men had expected, but they listened patiently. Ug explained that they would start again in the morning and head for the Village of No. None of the men were enthusiastic. Krat quit on the spot, without two weeks notice. Erf and Mug looked at Ug with bewilderment. They just experienced the most tremendous failure of their lives. Why would they want to do that again?

THE WORLD'S
FIRST SALESMAN

Ug told the men his new insight into this most important of sales techniques—You have to Properly Greet People. You have to greet them in a way that they'll want to talk with you. That was the missing ingredient. The men agreed that this was a good revelation, but they wondered if it was good enough to warrant another trip since the last one was such a failure.

Ug felt his own spirit and new enthusiasm wane. He had to do something, anything, to get these two on board with him. Krat was a quitter and he had no time for quitters, but these two were different. Just a short time ago they had really understood the vision of Ug Enterprises and the magical transformation that could occur in society with this new invention of the wheel. He decided to give them a speech, a pep talk like none other he'd or anyone he ever knew had ever given to anyone.

Ug began his speech with a resonant voice of conviction. Mug and Erf were astounded with the delivery. Never before had they heard a man speak so much from the heart with such belief, desire, drive, and power to enlighten others. Ug reminded them how the wheel was invented. How this new invention had already helped so many in their own village. How they had a duty to bring this new invention to all others in the world. How they would be great pioneers and be remembered for thousands of moons to come.

The men listened with attention and Erf had a tear in his eyes and enormous pride for his pal Ug filling his heart. Mug couldn't believe that the new eloquent words and sounds were coming from his own brother. A renewed sense of purpose washed over each man. They jumped in the air completely spirited by Ug's new powerful speech about motive power and innovation. Wait a minute... he was inventing something new once again... His powerful speech about motive and innovation, motive, innovation. Yes! Combine the words! Give a name to this type of speech—motive, innovation... MOTIVATION!!!! And that's what he called this new way of speaking, this new way of empowering others with the spirit of action— MOTIVATION!!!!

CHAPTER EIGHT

THE VILLAGE
OF NO

CHAPTER EIGHT

THE VILLAGE
OF NO

The Village of No lies a good three days from the foothills of the Valley of the Sun. No one in Ug's village was really sure what the name meant, but Ug and his friends would surely find out. With their newfound motivation and two loaded carts full of fabulous new wheels and axles, Ug, Erf, and Mug set out for the Village of No.

Ug was sure he could properly greet and make a connection with the people of No. In his mind he rehearsed his greeting over and over because he now knew that it was crucial to the success of his endeavor. He knew without a doubt that if he failed to create a favorable first impression with his greeting, he would never get to the next step.

The next step. "What was the next step?" Ug wondered. "Once I've given them a proper greeting, what do I do next?" Ug pondered this one question for the first full day and night of his journey to No.

Filled with angst for not knowing the next step, Ug

decided to put the question to his brethren, Erf and Mug. The three men sat resting under a shaded tree contemplating what to eat for their afternoon meal when Ug sprang the challenging question on his two younger companions. This created an arduous thought process for the three prehistoric men. At no time had anyone asked such a difficult question: What to do once they've made a proper greeting.

After hours of pondering this new dilemma and being determined to succeed at any cost, Ug decided on a two-step plan. First, they would show up in the Village of No and give a proper greeting. Then, they would ask to speak to the village leaders and show them the wheel. Perhaps these leaders would be bright enough to see the benefit of Ug's invention and offer food and other amenities to them in exchange for the wheels.

Late in the afternoon of their third day of travel, Erf smelled smoke coming from a clearing at the end of the woods. When they were closer, the three travelers could make out the smell of fresh meat being cooked. Their tummies growled with excitement. They hoped the people of No would be kind enough to share their dinner feast.

They approached the clearing in the woods. There were no caves, just rows of dome-like huts flanked by two very large huts. The huts were made of dried grass, leaves, twigs, and mud. "How inventive!" Ug thought. "If there aren't any caves available, you can use whatever is around you to make your own cave." Ug thought that perhaps the people of No were ingenious inventors, much like himself.

THE VILLAGE OF NO

As the three men pulled their carts through the wide clearing at the edge of the woods, they were stopped by four much larger men holding spears. One pointed his spear at Ug's throat and began to grunt. Ug, not understanding the language decided he better greet them in some effusive way to let them know that he and Erf and Mug were friendly travelers and meant no harm to the villagers of No. Ug pointed at the man's face. Immediately the man took on an angry look and lunged his spear at Ug, who in an instant fell to his knees to avoid the lunging spear.

Seeing Ug on his knees, all four of the men from No smiled, set their spears aside, and got onto their knees. They were speaking to Ug, Erf, and Mug now with smiles and warmth. Although Ug couldn't understand the language, he could tell that the danger had passed. Ug waved his hands on either side of him for Erf and Mug to also get down on their knees, which they did.

The four men from No were now laughing and smiling. They stood up and each embraced each one of the travelers. Obviously, getting on one's knees in the Village of No was the proper greeting. He laughed at their good fortune of figuring it out before it was too late. Erf and Mug were still somewhat shaken, but were relieved enough to join in the laughter. Soon all seven men were laughing as though a great joke had been told.

When they had finished their great laugh, Ug pointed to himself and then to the sky, which at that time was almost universally understood as the sign for "Take me to your leader." The tallest of the four men from No nodded in agreement, and all seven men set off for the center of the village where a large feast was being prepared.

As they approached, the men, women, and children of No looked with awe at these strangers. One man looked into Ug's eyes with a distrustful glare. At that moment, Ug tried out his new etiquette and dropped to his knees and smiled. The man's face immediately changed to show warmth and understanding, and he too dropped to his knees and smiled.

"This is great," Ug thought. "I now understand exactly how to greet the people of No." Then Ug began to worry that he needed a cleverer next step. And what if he couldn't convince any of them to get the wheels? "Try not to think of that right now," he told himself. "Enjoy the moment."

The men walked through the village, occasionally dropping to their knees to greet villagers and newfound friends. They came upon a group of five other men, all seemed to be middle aged—not the youngest in the village and certainly not the oldest. The original four men that greeted Ug and his crew all nodded goodbye and parted, leaving Ug, Erf, and Mug with the five new men they had just met. All eight men fell to their knees in greeting and all eight men arose from their knees laughing and smiling. One of the men made a motion with his hands and mouth and then grabbed his belly. He was inviting Ug and his men to supper and they heartily accepted.

Ug, Erf, and Mug were treated to a feast of perfectly prepared gazelle meat with generous helpings of wild boar.

After dinner, one of the five men gestured for Ug and his men to follow him. They walked to another part of the village to meet yet another group, this time of six men, from No. These men seemed a bit older than the last five, but Ug could tell they were not the oldest and wisest of the village. The men treated Ug, Erf, and Mug to a tangy liquid. It was definitely not water, which was the only liquid that Ug and his men had ever consumed. This liquid was tangy, almost spicy, and made Ug feel at first a little dizzy and then a little woozy.

After consuming several vessels of the liquid, all of the men were intoxicated. Ug had never felt such joy and love for his fellow man. Despite their language differences, all nine men were laughing, smiling, and having a grand time.

Ug held up his vessel and patted one of the men from No on the shoulder while gesturing towards the vessel filled with the pungent liquid.

The man pointed and said, "Wine."

Whatever it was Ug knew for sure he had found what he wanted, something new and exciting to take back to his own village in exchange for the wheels.

After a few hours of drinking, laughing, and feeling absolutely no pain whatsoever, the six men from No stood up. As five of them nodded goodbye to their new friends from the Valley of the Sun, one man gestured for Ug, Erf, and Mug to follow. This man led them to yet another part of the village, where there were now seven men, definitely older than the last six men, who were waiting to greet Ug,

THE WORLD'S
FIRST SALESMAN

Erf, and Mug. One of the new men made a gesture with his hands that appeared to be sleeping. Ug instantly understood and nodded agreement. The seven men then stood up and six of them parted while one man led Ug, Erf, and Mug to an empty hut. He gestured for the weary travelers to go inside, make themselves at home, and get a good night's rest.

Just before he drifted off to sleep, Ug felt a great sense of accomplishment. He was awash with joy over the day's events and was looking forward to the next day when he would certainly have a chance to market his wares. He was confident he would prevail.

The next morning, Ug awoke feeling refreshed and ready to take on the challenges that lay before him. He stood up and stretched, grunting loudly while he did to awake the others. He peeked his head out of the hut and saw the same man that led them to the hut the night before.

The man smiled and approached Ug. He patted Ug on the top of the head in a friendly gesture. Then the man patted himself on the chest and grunted a word that sounded like "Bok." Ug patted himself on the chest and said, "Ug." The two men nodded in acknowledgement to one another.

Two of the village women came to the hut. One was carrying a large vessel of fresh water, and the other presented Ug with a large bowl of freshly picked berries. Ug had never seen this type of sustenance. However, after the experience from the night before, Ug realized that these people meant no harm. He was sure it was safe to try the berries.

Ug took a fist full of berries and shoved them into

his mouth. All of a sudden he experienced a delicious sensation, like none other he'd ever tasted. One moment he experienced a tart flavor and then the flavor turned sweet and syrupy in his mouth. "Wow," he thought. "These people from No really know how to live."

Excited by the blissed-out expression on Ug's face, Erf and Mug each took a handful. Erf commented that these berries should be brought back to their village in exchange for the wheels. Mug agreed and said they should also bring back a lot of that funny "wine" they had the previous night. Ug realized that the new fruit they were eating tasted a little like the wine they had the night before.

After a healthy breakfast of berries, some leftover gazelle meat, and lots of water, the three men were ready to start their businesses day. Ug motioned to Bok that he wanted to know where his carts were. Bok made a motion with his hands indicating a long beard, which told Ug that his carts were with the village elder. Bok then made a motion showing the cart and with his hands defined a wheel. He then pointed to his head. At first Ug thought the man was saying that Ug was crazy for making a wheel. Ug grew visibly flushed with anger. Erf, taking account of this, elbowed Ug. He explained that he thought Bok was saying that the invention was the work of genius. Ug then smiled in affirmation and nodded a humble thank you at Bok. Bok smiled back.

Bok led the men to yet another part of the village. In this part of the village, many young men and women were working, gutting gazelles and boars for fresh meat and stock piling water and berries. Two large animals helped move some of the heavier loads. Ug had never seen these animals before. When he gestured, Bok said, "Oxen." He noticed how well the people worked with the animals. It was as though they were a team—the people and the animals working together. He mulled over this concept again and again in his mind—the team and the work, the people and the team and the work. How fascinating. The team and the work. Team. Work. Team, work—TEAMWORK!

Ug was astounded with the amount of new things, new food, new drink, and new innovations he found here in the Village of No. He realized that his own villagers could learn a lot from these wonderful people. Although Ug held himself now in high esteem as a worldly inventor, he realized that there were many others like him in the world, particularly here in No.

Bok led the men into a large hut on the far perimeter of the village, completely opposite the side of the village where Ug, Erf, and Mug had their nights sleep. Inside the hut stood a new group of men, eight in all, who were certainly older than the last seven men they met the previous night. Inside the hut was one of the carts filled with wheels and axles. Upon entering the hut, Erf, Mug, and Ug immediately dropped to their knees. The eight men followed suit. The men then rose and embraced each one of the travelers. Ug, Mug, and Erf felt absolute joy. At each new meeting within this fascinating village, the welcome was even warmer and friendlier than the last.

One man stepped forward and pounded his own

chest and uttered a word that sounded like, "Jok." Jok made a gesture towards one of the wheels and then pointed to his head and smiled. Jok was signifying "genius." He then pointed questioningly towards Ug. Ug smiled and nodded in affirmation. Yes, he was indeed the inventor of the wheel.

Jok then motioned for Ug and his men to give a demonstration. Erf grabbed an axle from the cart and laid it on the floor of the hut, in the middle of the circle formed by the No villagers. Mug and Ug each grabbed a wheel. Erf lifted the axle while Mug and Ug fastened the wheels to each end of the axle. Erf then pushed the axle forward and then pulled it backward showing the motion of the wheels and the axle. The three men looked around the room to see eight pairs of astonished eyes and eight wide smiles.

The No men conversed amongst themselves. This lasted for several minutes. When the huddle broke, Jok approached Ug. Jok placed his hand on the smaller man's shoulder, gazed into his eyes, and made a gesture like stroking a beard, signifying that he would bring Ug and his men to the real village elders, the wisest men in the village!

Ug nodded in agreement. Erf and Mug began to disassemble the wheels and axle, when one of Jok's men grunted for their attention and told them to stop. At first Erf, Mug, and Ug were worried that perhaps these men were going to confiscate their wares without a fair trade. But the man made a gesture of stroking a beard and then pointed to the cart letting the travelers know that the real village elders had in their possession the other cart. For the sake of expedience, they should leave this cart and return for it

---

later. Ug, Mug, and Erf understood and followed Jok out of the hut.

At the elders' hut, there were nine men with gray beards waiting for them. These were certainly the village elders. After the customary greeting, Jok excused himself and left the hut. The second cart was in the center of the hut. Ug, Mug, and Erf repeated the demonstration they had given to the previous group of men. The nine elders of No were certainly impressed. One of them grunted and a very old and very wise looking man entered the room. It was clear to Ug that this man indeed was the oldest and wisest of the elders.

The man looked Ug up and down. It occurred to Ug that letting the old man go first with the greeting would be a sign of disrespect. So Ug gestured to Mug and Erf to properly greet the elder, which all three did together. The old and wise man also dropped to his knees and then slowly rose to his feet. The old man patted his own chest and stated his name, "Rap." Ug responded with theirs. Then Rap turned his attention to the wheel, gesturing for yet another demonstration, which the three foreigners enthusiastically provided.

Rap stroked his beard and gazed upon the new invention with an intense and calculating look. He gestured for one of his men to bring him a stick. Rap had the men form a circle around him and drew a diagram of the cart in the dirt. He then shocked the others with his keen understanding and insight and drew a team of oxen connected to the cart. All of the twelve men standing in a circle nodded

CHAPTER EIGHT
THE VILLAGE OF NO

in understanding. Ug, the great inventor, had just seen his invention greatly improved with the addition of a team of oxen. A light bulb went on inside Ug's head, but then he quickly dismissed it realizing that the light bulb would not be invented for many centuries.

Rap was not through with his drawing. Soon there were trees and lines indicating how the ox driven carts could be used to bring heavy building supplies from the woods. He further diagrammed expansion plans for new hut developments in the Village of No. All the men were greatly impressed. At that moment Ug received the thumbs up from Rap to deliver his first order of wheels. Ug was blown away! Rap indicated that all of the wheels in the cart and all of the wheels in the other cart should remain in the Village of No. He then asked what Ug wanted in exchange. Mug was blurting out the word "wine" while Erf was making a gesture that looked like eating berries. And so it was agreed—wine and berries for wheels and axels. Inter-village commerce was created.

To seal the deal, Rap had a feast brought into the hut and all thirteen men ate, celebrated, and drank wine together. After a few hours of celebration, Rap approached Ug and put his arm around him. Rap pointed to himself and said, "port." At first Ug looked a little dumbfounded. Recognizing the younger man's dilemma, Rap embraced Ug. When he let go, he pointed to Ug and himself and said the word again, "port." This time Ug understood. In the Village of No, the word "port" meant "friend." Rap was his friend. Rap, Port. Rap friend, Rap Port—RAPPORT. Ug knew the crucial second step of his selling process: Make a friend of the client or, using his new term, BUILD RAPPORT!!!

Mug, Ug, and Erf left the Village of No very happy and with two carts filled with berries, wine, and some gutted gazelle to eat on their journey home. As they ended the first day of their return travels, they decided to make camp under a tree by a babbling brook. With the campfire built and the gazelle before them, they all agreed it had been a fabulous trip. They decided they would celebrate their great accomplishment, and so they tore the heads off a few of the wine vessels and drank themselves into a happy stupor. Ug told his men his revelation about the next step in the process of selling wheels—this new concept he called Building Rapport. The men all agreed that, in order to trade wheels for other goods, it was important first to perform a Proper Greeting and then to establish Rapport with the prospect.

Then Ug wondered aloud how many of the No villagers they had actually encountered. First they met 4, then 5, then 6, then 7, then 8 then 9, and 1. Well, that was 40 No villagers. That was a tremendous amount of Nos. He realized that perhaps that's just the way it is sometimes; you sometimes have to go through a lot of Noes in order to get the order.

CHAPTER NINE

THE TRIP TO QUALI MOUNTAIN

CHAPTER NINE

THE TRIP TO QUALI MOUNTAIN

When Ug, Mug, and Erf returned to the Valley of the Sun, they were given a true hero's welcome. The villagers had never seen nor tasted such wonders as the wine and berries and were astounded that such goodies existed in the world outside of their own village.

Feeling stupid for doubting his friend Ug, Krat asked for his job back. Ug agreed but told Krat he would have to start back as a laborer, making wheels and axles. Other villagers approached Ug and asked how they could be part of this great new enterprise. Ug decided he could put several people to work making wheels and that he could pay them in berries and wine. Although this meant that all of the profits would be consumed, he knew that it made sense at this stage of his new venture to reinvest the profits back into the business.

And so several more villagers were put to work at Ug Enterprises, which did business as The International Wheel and Axle Company, or IWAC. Ug put Pung to work as a production supervisor and soon they were turning out nearly three new wheels and two axles a day. After a few weeks of production, the supply of berries and wine was running out. Ug realized that he and his men had better make their next journey to trade more wheels for other goodies.

Ug looked at his stockpiles of wheels and axles and realized that far more wheels and axles were produced than could fit in two carts. He saw that he had an inventory backlog and soon would not be able to pay his employees. It was time to act. They assembled two more carts to carry the surplus. This time he had to take 5 more men, using 2 to pull each cart. Perhaps they would encounter some oxen during their next trip.

To determine their next destination, Ug decided to consult with Al, the village elder. Al named a few places and suggested that the men could see all of them in one trip. These places were the mountain Village of Quali, the Land of Ob, and the waterfront Village of Nah. Ug took the plan back to his men, and they agreed to venture out the very next day.

At sun up the next morning, Ug, Mug, Erf, Pung, Krat, Gork, Mup, and Pung's son, Pong all set out with four carts loaded with wheels and axles. Attempting to see 3 different villages on one trip was Ug's biggest venture yet.

After four days of difficult travel, the men encountered a steep mountainous path of dirt, gravel and the occasional boulder. Al had described this as the way to the mountain Village of Quali. Erf stared nervously at Ug. Did

THE TRIP TO QUALI MOUNTAIN

Ug really want the men to lug the carts all the way up this steep mountain path? Ug realized this would be quite a chore for two men pulling one cart, and so he made an executive decision. They would leave two carts behind, hoping they would be there when the men returned, and they would use four men to pull each of two carts up the mountain.

The men started the upward trek. Ug, Pung, Krat, and Pong led the way with the first cart and were followed by Mup, Erf, Gork, and Mug on the second. The men pulled each cart with all of their might. Ug could feel the burning in his legs from the strenuous pull. His team was sweating profusely, but they were making good progress.

All of a sudden Pung tripped on a rock, fell hard, and let go of the vine he used to pull the cart. The other men on his team tried hard to keep from slipping, but the cart was too heavy and the hill was too steep. As Ug, Krat, and Pong held tightly to the vines, the cart began to roll backwards, taking the remaining three men with it.

Mug, who was leading the second team, saw what was happening and quickly ordered his men to park their cart in front of a large boulder to keep it from rolling backwards while they attempted to help the first team. But it was too late. Ug's cart was now rolling so fast that the three men were forced to let go for their own safety. All eight men watched in horror as the careening cart smashed into a large boulder at the base of the hill and shattered into several pieces.

The men stood on the hillside in silence, unsure of what to do next. Pung apologized to the group for losing his footing and allowing the cart to give way. Ug realized that his decision to have four men pull each cart up the hill was overzealous and he should never have attempted it. It's just too heavy, and now one of his carts was destroyed.

Although the loss was devastating, it was not enough to keep Ug and his men from continuing on their journey. At least now, perhaps, the trip up to the mountainous Village of Quali would be more bearable.

Although Ug and his men could see the outskirts of the village from the base of the mountain, the trip up to it took almost two days. They camped for the night about halfway up to the village. By the late afternoon on their second day of uphill travel, the entrepreneurs from the Valley of the Sun finally made it to the outer reaches of the Village of Quali.

Two men from Quali came to greet Ug and his men. They spoke in the same language that Ug and his people spoke in the Valley of the Sun. This was astonishing to Ug and the others. Ug guessed that since they used the same language, these villagers might also use the same greeting. So Ug, being the competent statesman and leader of his group, help out his hand and told the men that he was Ug, from the Valley of the Sun.

"Aha!" exclaimed one of the men as he took Ug's hand. He introduced himself as "Krok" and his associate as "Tok." Krok asked Ug what business he had in the Village of Quali. Ug explained that he had traveled a long way across the plains and up the mountain because he had a new invention he wanted to share with the people of Quali.

THE TRIP TO QUALI MOUNTAIN

Krok nodded his understanding and told Ug that since they had journeyed so far, this new invention must be very important. Ug and his men should enter the village at once and join Krok and his men for some food. Later Krok would assemble all of the people of the village to see this great new invention. Krok led the way, which was still uphill. Ug and his men followed with the cart.

Realizing that he already had begun the selling process by giving a Proper Greeting, Ug decided that now would be a good time to start Building Rapport with Krok. So Ug asked how it was that the people of Quali could possibly be speaking the same language as the people from the Valley of the Sun.

Krok explained with a story. "You see, Ug, a long, long time ago, in the far off land known as the Valley of Meat near the Stream of Life was a village known as the Village of Pre-Quali. The villagers lived there in harmony with nature and with plenty of food all around them. The village was a thriving sprawl with many families and lots of activity.

"Each autumn the rains would come and the river would flow wildly. One very sad autumn the rains came, as they usually do, but this time they did not let up. It rained and rained and continued to rain until one day the banks of the Stream of Life overflowed into the Valley of Meat. Many of the Pre-Qualians were lost during the great flood. At that time, there was a village elder named Karik who urged all of the people to uproot from the village and move the Pre-Qualian civilization to higher ground in

---

the mountains.

"Most of the villagers agreed, except for a young pioneer named Zug. Zug agreed that the surviving villagers needed to move to higher ground, but believed that moving to the mountains could be too treacherous and there might not be enough food up there to sustain them. Zug, his wife Tara, their children, Zug's brother Thug and his wife and children, and a few other villagers decided to make their way to the Valley of the Sun. It was agreed that if the Pre-Quali villagers could not survive in the mountains, they would come down and reside in the Valley of the Sun. That was many, many moons ago. As you can see, we have survived and thrived here for all of these years."

Ug was fascinated. He knew that many moons ago his ancestor, Zug had founded their village in the Valley of the Sun, but the rest of the story was new. Ug asked how many villagers from Pre-Quali were lost during this great flood.

"Legend has it that about half of the villagers were lost at that time," responded Krok.

Both men were silent as they pondered this sad fate. Then Ug said, "I've visited the Valley of Meat several times but am not aware of a stream known as the Stream of Life."

"The Stream of Life was renamed. It is now known as the Stream of Ghosts because so many people were lost to the stream during that great flood."

Despite the sad story, Ug felt a friendship forming with Krok due to this strong ancestral bond they uncovered. He looked forward to meeting the other villagers, who were also possible relations, and demonstrating his great invention.

Krok continued to lead the men uphill. They passed several huts. These were manmade caves somewhat like the ones he saw in No, but these were made of rocks instead of grass and tree branches. "There's a whole world of innovation out there," thought Ug. He knew his invention would only add to it.

Finally, the men came to a level plateau. The level area was not very large at all, only about the length of thirty paces and the width of twenty. Surrounding the small plateau area were benches made of rocks and large tree branches. This was a gathering area for the villagers. Ug wondered where they all were. He looked around and noticed that the manmade caves continued up the mountain for some distance, almost as far as he could see.

Krok let out a loud whistle and from further up the mountain, three women appeared carrying large bowls of food. Several men also appeared carrying large wooden tables and many more villagers came streaming down the mountain. Within a few minutes, a large feast was laid in the gathering area. Krok introduced Ug and his men to the villagers. The men warmly greeted and freely mingled with the villagers who were probably long lost relatives of theirs.

The feast was wonderful. They ate a different kind of meat than Ug or any of his men had ever tasted. Unlike the thick bones and brown meat of the gazelles and wild boar that they were used to, this meat was white and attached to very skinny bones. Ug didn't know what it was, but he liked the taste. Krok told him it was the meat of wild birds that the villagers caught with traps created out of twigs and vines. Ug was astounded. He never knew that you could eat birds. He and his men enjoyed the hearty feast, which included wild berries—delicious but different from the ones he had in No.

As the sun sank below the mountainside, Krok stood up in the middle of the crowded gathering place and made a speech to all in attendance. It was clear from Krok's speech that he was the leader of this village. There were several older men in attendance, but, unlike most villages, the elders sat back and let the younger man take charge. Krok began by telling the story he told Ug of how the villagers of Pre-Quali long ago left their homes and split their village between the Valley of the Sun and the Village of Quali. Krok told the people of Quali that these men were long lost relatives and that Ug was an inventor with a great invention to share with the Qualians.

Krok turned the meeting over to Ug, who introduced himself and his men. Erf and Mug unloaded and assembled an axle and wheel set while Ug told the story of his great invention. When the wheels were assembled, Mug and Erf rolled them around inside the gathering area. Ug's other men then pulled the cart into the center of the gathering area. Ug told the villagers how this great invention could help them in gathering, hunting, and carrying their loot. He also told them how a team of oxen could pull a cart made with these new wheels.

Ug looked at the villagers. They were bewildered.

THE TRIP TO QUALI MOUNTAIN

Ug hoped that they were simply awestruck at the genius of his invention. He didn't know what else to do so he went for the deal. He told the villagers that he would trade three carts of wheels and axles for two carts of berries and one cart of bird meat.

The villagers looked even more perplexed. One man stood up and said he didn't see why they should give any of their berries and birds to the men from the Valley of the Sun for just a few carts full of round discs. Others jumped in and voiced the same opinion. As their bewilderment turned to agitation, Krok stepped in and calmed them down. Krok reminded them that these men were their friends and distant relatives, and they should be treated as such. He then dismissed the crowd.

He called to Ug and his men to join him inside his manmade cave, which was just off the main village gathering area. Inside, he explained the reaction of the other villagers. You see, they didn't see the value or use in Ug's new invention because their village was scattered throughout the mountainside. Using a cart with Ug's new wheels just wouldn't work in Quali. Krok acknowledged that Ug's invention was indeed a very good one but only for villagers that lived on flatter ground where the carts could be easily pulled or pushed on wheels.

With great disappointment in himself for not having grasped this sooner, Ug thanked Krok for his explanation. Ug apologized for causing such a stir and then, to his own men, for pushing them up the mountain only to realize that these villagers had no use for the product. Krok had the men stay in his cave for the night, so they could rest up well before they took the next leg of their journey.

As the men slowly and quietly headed down the mountain the next morning, Ug felt an emptiness in his heart. He should have known! He should have realized that this particular village wasn't a good prospect for his invention.

Ug had just learned a lesson he would not soon forget. Before you travel for many moons to show your product, make sure the customer has a need for it. The customer must be able to specify a use. He muttered aloud, "The Qualians simply couldn't specify a use for this invention. The Village of Quali couldn't specify... Quali, specify, qual specify, qualspecify, qual-ify..." He needed a word to remind him of this lesson. "He must quali-fy, QUALIFY!!!!!" And thus the third part of the puzzle was identified: You must Qualify the prospect.

CHAPTER TEN

THE LAND OF OB

CHAPTER TEN

THE LAND OF OB

Once Ug and his men returned to flatter land at the base of Quali Mountain, Ug informed his men that, although they encountered defeat this time, they would surely have success again soon. He told them, "Just like you, I am disappointed and tired, but in order to be successful in this new business, we must persist. If the villagers of No wanted this invention, so certainly will others. We only have to make sure that these new prospects are qualified."

Predictably, Krat grew angry and quit again. He decided to make the return trip alone back to the Valley of the Sun. Ug told Krat that because this was the second time he was quitting, he would not be eligible for rehire. Krat coldly told Ug he didn't care and took off in an indignant huff, heading back to the Valley of the Sun.

The rest of the men still believed in Ug, but their enthusiasm was certainly less than it had been before the long trek to Quali. Ug decided it was time once again to practice motivation and to re-energize his remaining men. He had the men sit around in a circle near the base of a large shady tree. He stood in the middle and delivered his second motivational speech.

Ug told the men that they were all pioneers of industry and that one day the world would be a better place because they had made the wheel available for all "qualified" civilizations everywhere. He explained that one day villages would be everywhere, from Quali Mountain, deep into the Valley of Meat, and far past the Stream of Ghosts. He asked his men to imagine a future when more than a thousand people, all using their wheels, were living better lives because of them, the early pioneers of the International Wheel and Axle Company. He instilled his vision of growing to a very large, multi-village company with branch offices in places like Grump, No, and even Ob.

Ug closed his motivation speech by telling the men that more important than the discovery of the wheel was the contribution they were making to the foundation of enterprise by building a system for convincing others to acquire new and valuable goods. Yes, he reminded them, they were pioneers, heroes, who would be known throughout the world for many generations.

With renewed excitement and commitment, the men cheered. Equally energized and committed, Ug promised that he was determined not to fail. He would succeed at all costs. He would travel as many moons as was necessary to make the wheel an internationally excepted and utilized invention. The men cheered again. They were with him all the way.

Ug then reviewed what they had learned so far about being successful in commerce. First, they had to identify and execute a good and Proper Greeting. Next, they needed to Establish Rapport. And then, of course, they had to Qualify their prospect. He knew there was more to the puzzle and was determined to figure out what that next step should be on the way to Ob.

After a few additional minutes of rest and excited conversation, the men gathered the unbroken wheels from their lost cart, loaded them in the three remaining carts, and began the journey east towards the Land of Ob.

While walking, Ug engaged his top advisers Erf and Mug, who were now elevated to executive status in Ug's company, on the question of what they thought the next step should be in the process of marketing their wares. The first three steps of the selling process were now crystal clear. He asked them to think about what the next natural step would be in the event that they were able to Greet Properly, Establish Rapport, and Qualify the prospect. Erf yawned to hide his confusion. Mug simply stared at the sky.

"Big help these guys are," thought Ug.

Just then Mug tapped Ug on the shoulder and pointed up at a flock of geese flying in close formation high above and to the northeast of where the men were walking. They looked so majestic all flying in such symmetry. If only all things could be so well formed in business. If only Ug and his men could be in such great formation when they went to see a new customer.

The men continued on their way. Ug, Erf, and Mug pulled the first cart and Pung and Pong pulled the second. Gork and Mup brought up the rear with the third. Ug couldn't shake the sight or the idea of the beautifully organized grouping of geese. He imagined the geese must have a plan that they practice from time to time so their flight would look so well orchestrated to those that observed them.

The idea of being well organized and well planned stuck with Ug. Perhaps that was the way to bring about a desired result—to be well planned and organized. He and his men should do this. They should plan every visit well before they first greet their potential prospects. Ug feared that if they were not well organized on each visit, other villages might reject their offer, even if they were qualified—even if they did need the product. That was an interesting revelation to Ug. It could actually be possible that others would reject their offer, even if they truly needed the product. It happened in Grump simply because they did not know how to properly greet the people of Grump. Surely it could happen elsewhere.

Ug realized he needed a solution to this new dilemma. The wheel was impractical for the people of Quali, but what if they meet other people who live on flatter ground but can't imagine how the invention could help them. What if Ug could see that it would clearly change their lives for the better, but they themselves couldn't? Obviously, he would have to specify the use for them and present it to them. The trick would be to get them to understand and agree.

"Now how does that fit with the majestic flight of the geese?" he thought aloud.

All of a sudden, like a lightening bolt from the sky striking Ug's head, he got it. He knew what had to be done. He thanked the gods of the trees, water, and food for this wonderful realization. He now knew that, if you could specify someone else's needs, then, like the majestic flight of the geese, you could organize your entire conversation around those needs and how the invention would fulfill them. Instead of waiting for the prospect to figure it out, you could determine what their needs are or what their expectations are for such a product and present those needs and expectations and their solutions to the prospect as a gift. You could give them a present that would solve their needs. Interesting concept! Present expectations, presentexpectations, present-pectations, presentations, PRESENTATION! And thus, inspired by geese, was born the next step in the commerce process. The well planned, well orchestrated, and majestic Presentation.

Ob was a prehistoric village located two moons northeast from Quali Mountain. Legend has it that Ob was the oldest and perhaps the first village ever established in the world, and its people were the most advanced of all peoples. These tall tales did not discourage Ug because he believed that his invention of the wheel put the Valley of the Sun on the map as an innovative people to be reckoned with—an advanced civilization.

THE WORLD'S
FIRST SALESMAN

Late on the second day of their journey from Quali Mountain, the travelers could see the outskirts of Ob dotting the valley at the base of the hill the men were traversing. Night was falling fast and the men all agreed it would not be wise to approach Ob in the darkness, so they made camp at the top of the hill overlooking Ob.

Ug reflected upon the past two days and his new concept of the Presentation. He knew that he was on the cusp of a discovery that was equal to or even greater than the wheel. He was elated at life and the opportunity to take on new challenges. He was amazed by his own strength to overcome great obstacles. Somehow he was becoming a new man, and he felt a certain responsibility for society and the furtherance of the human race. He knew he was only at the very beginning of a great journey in life that would lead to many great things. The wheel was just the start.

As he stared up at the stars hanging brilliantly in the pitch-dark sky, Ug had a vision. He saw himself as someone who was destined for greatness, not because of his invention of the wheel but for some other divine purpose. He knew then that there was a reason he was born to this earth. He only needed to figure out what that divine purpose was. Perhaps, he thought, he was already on the journey to find out. He pitied those villagers that lived only to hunt, kill, eat, sleep, and otherwise lie around the cave doing nothing. What a meager life. One could be out doing great things, not just letting the time waste away. To be truly alive, Man must have a dream. He must have a vision of what is possible and the motivation to go after it.

THE LAND OF OB

While dreaming about his own future, Ug fell into a peaceful, relaxing sleep on the grassy hill overlooking the Land of Ob.

At first glance, Ob was the most fascinating village the men had yet encountered. The men watched as the village came alive with men and women performing chores, children playing, and animals walking amongst the villagers. Erf tapped Ug on the shoulder and pointed to the animals. Ug nodded. There were two types of animals they had never seen. One was short and fat and had a thick wooly coat. The other was large and heavy with a smooth hide. What was surprising was that these animals were alive and walking amongst the villagers. The men all wondered if you could eat them.

As their thoughts drifted to imagining how these animals might taste, their hunger grew. They decided to try their luck with the villagers rather than hunting new food. The plan was that Ug and Erf would approach the villagers alone and on foot to establish friendly relations. Everyone agreed that this was a good plan, but Pung, always the hungriest of the group, stressed that Ug and Erf needed to hurry or Pung might die of starvation. Ug rolled his eyes in the universal and timeless symbol for "Whatever!"

Ug and Erf set out to make their way down the hill with the others watching impatiently. If the villagers were friendly and accommodating, Ug or Erf would wave the others down. If the villagers were unfriendly or worse yet, violent, then Ug and Erf would be sacrificed so the others could escape and make their way back to the Valley of

---

the Sun.

Upon reaching the base of the hill, Ug and Erf were immediately accosted by two young men with spears. It was a frightening site and Erf immediately thought they should attempt to run back up the hill. Ug realized that an escape attempt would be futile as these two young men appeared to be in top shape, probably champion meat tossers and hunters.

One man poked Ug with the spear. Not enough to pierce the skin, but enough for Ug to feel the sharpness and be very intimidated.

"Awa?" asked the young spear carrying native of Ob. "Awa dhaba?" Not understanding the language, Ug could not answer.

"Awa dhaba macaba?" the sentry asked, this time quite angrily.

Ug threw his hands straight up in the air in a gesture to show that he did not understand the communication.

"Awa dhaba macaba? Awa dhaba macaba?" This time he was shouting at the top of his lungs.

Ug made the same gesture and this time the young sentry held the spear like a baseball bat and swiftly swung at Ug's legs. Ug jumped over the spear as it neared its destined contact point. The young sentry looked at Ug and said, "Hmm?"

The sentry took another swipe at Ug's legs, and Ug jumped over the stick again. This time the sentry laughed. So did his companion. But the companion still held his spear close to the heart of Erf.

THE LAND OF OB

From high above on the hillside, Pong, Gork, Mup, Mug, and Pung surveyed the situation and were deep in conference. Should they fight to save their associates or flee as they had originally agreed? The decision was made. They only saw two sentries and there were five of them, plus Ug and Erf—seven in total against two. It would be a rout.

Gork, Mug, Mup, and Pung strategized that they would slowly make their way down the hillside, being careful not to be seen. Pong would stay behind and once the other four were in position, Pong would let one of the carts roll down the hill, creating a diversion. Once the sentries were distracted, Pung and Gork would take out one sentry and Mup and Mug would take down the other. The men were certain that this was a brilliant plan. The four men made their way down the hill.

The sentry continued to swipe at Ug's legs and Ug continued to jump over the stick, each time provoking a loud laugh from the sentry. The other sentry laughed as well. Swipe, jump, laugh, swipe jump laugh. Although Ug's life was in danger, he was beginning to laugh, too. Just then all four men heard a loud rumbling noise. It was the cart lumbering down the hillside. Both sentries looked on in wonder. Ug lunged at his sentry and grabbed the spear from his hands, taking control over the younger man. Erf shifted his body around the other sentry's spear, moved in close, and punched the man in the nose. The two sentries were stunned by the swiftness of their disarmament. Just then the cart rolled by all of them and continued to make its way into the village.

Immediately following the cart were the charging screams of Ug's four other men, who, to their amazement, found their companions now in charge of the situation. All eight men watched in silence as the cart careened into the village and straight towards a large thatched hut.

The sentry who was now under the guard of Ug brought his hands to his face reddened by extreme embarrassment. He yelled, "Oy lalalala, Oh Vey!"

The other sentry joined in. "Oy Vey, Oy Vey!!!!!"

As the cart slammed into what appeared to be the largest and nicest hut in the village, it knocked a hole clean through and eventually collapsed the hut. Stunned villagers looked on in amazement. Standing in the middle of the wreckage, was a large, burly man with lots of war paint. He was screaming at the villagers and pointing towards the base of the hill where Ug, his men, and the two sentries were stunned into silence.

"We've gotten into a mighty fine mess this time," Ug thought.

The villagers grabbed spears and ran towards Ug's men, making escape impossible. Pong stood alone on the hillside watching the debacle. Although he was the youngest of the crew, Pong was a brave and quick-witted young soul. He realized that if he didn't act swiftly, he would soon witness the rapid death of all his comrades. He grabbed the wheels out of the remaining two carts and rolled them down the hill in the direction of the armed villagers. The first wheel was about to make a direct hit of one of the Ob villagers. He jumped out of the way but fell down. On his

THE LAND OF OB

way down, he grazed another villager behind him, knocking him down as well. That villager fell into another and so on until a chain reaction was created that knocked down nine of the ten flanking villagers.

Quite impressed with himself, Pong thought about what a fun game this would be if his friends weren't fighting for their lives right now. He decided that he could be an inventor just like Ug, and, if he lived through this fiasco, he would create a game just like this. Coming back to his senses, he rolled another wheel down the hill toward another group of Ob villagers who were flanking Pong's friends on the other side. This time he knocked down six men. He followed up with another wheel to the same side and three more men fell. By this time most of the men on the other side were back on their feet. He sent another wheel down the hill, but this time the men were prepared, and they all safely got out of the way.

Pong knew that his strategy had only a temporary effect. Now it appeared that all of his friends were doomed. But just then the large man from the destroyed hut appeared to intervene. He walked straight towards Ug and his men. Oddly enough, the man was laughing. In fact, he was laughing really hard as he pointed to the first group that Pong had knocked down.

The man laughed and laughed and then said, "Boom" and made a gesture as though falling down himself. He was obviously quite amused with the ease and proficiency with which Pong had made all of his men fall down with just the roll of one wheel.

THE WORLD'S
FIRST SALESMAN

The laughing man approached Ug, who was still holding the spear at the heart of his younger assailant. The man confidently pushed the point of the spear down towards the ground and away from the heart of the young sentry. He was still laughing as he raised his hands towards both flanking groups of villagers in a gesture to stop their approaches. He looked into Ug's eyes and patted his own chest with his right hand and said, "Bonga." He then made a waiving motion towards the village and said, "Ob." Bonga then touched Ug's chest and asked, "Etu?"

Ug, who had become more astute and worldly in the art of understanding gestures and greetings touched his own chest and said, "Ug."

Bonga responded with a nod and repeated, "Ug." He waived out into the distance and asked, "Macaba?"

Ug still wasn't sure exactly what the question meant. He assumed because the man pointed to his own village and said the name of it that perhaps he was asking what village Ug was from. So Ug replied, "Valley of the Sun."

"Ahhhhh," Bonga said. "Valley Sun! Ahhhhhhh." He gestured for one of the younger, faster sentries to come hither. "Baba gaga Kanush! Baba gaga Kanush," he yelled to the young man. The young man sprinted towards the village.

The word 'Kanush' was familiar to Ug—not as a word but as a name. Kanush was a villager from the Valley of the Sun who, as a very young man, had had a theory that there was life in other villages. This was before Ug's time but legend had it that Kanush set out on his own to prove to the skeptical villagers of the Valley of the Sun that there was indeed life in other villages. If he were still alive today, Kanush would be far older than even Al, the village elder. The story went that Kanush never returned because he walked to the end of the earth and fell off into the abyss.

Bonga, obviously the village leader, continued to laugh about the fallen sentries and the way in which Pong accomplished this feat. Bonga gestured for Pong to come down the hill and join the others. Unconvinced that the danger had passed, Pong was reluctant to give up such a strategically effective position so he held his ground.

The fast running sentry returned, this time walking very slowly and holding onto a frail and very old man with long streaming white hair. The old man was very small and looked as though he would fall apart if the wind blew. Ug knew he was standing in the presence of a legend.

Kanush looked up at Ug with squinty eyes, put his right hand on his own chest, and said, "I am Kanush. I am from the Valley of the Sun." Ug and his men were all speechless. Ug guessed that Kanush might be as old as fifty, a feat rarely accomplished in any village. Kanush could be the oldest living man on earth.

Once Ug came to his senses, he put his own right hand on his own chest and said, "Ug. I am also from the Valley of the Sun."

The older man moved forward with tears in his eyes and embraced the younger Ug. "You are Ug, son of Pug, grandson of Lug of the Valley of the Sun."

Wow, thought Ug. This was a new magnificent

chapter in his journey. Ug could not believe what an incredible story this would be to tell his fellow villagers once he returned home.

Bonga looked at Kanush, pointed at Ug, and asked, "Awa dhaba macaba?"

Kanush translated, "Bonga is the village leader. He wants to know what brought you and your men here to our village."

Ug explained about his journey and his incredible new invention. Kanush then interpreted for Bonga and Bonga nodded in understanding. Bonga then made a gesture like a knife going across a throat and said, "Kowa bonga malinga. Magunga tawinga pulinga, ha ha!"

Interpreting for Ug, Kanush said, "You are very lucky you are not dead. But you made the big man laugh. He loves to laugh. So he will spare your life."

Ug asked Kanush to thank the big man, which Kanush did interpret for him. Bonga smiled broadly, the international sign of "all clear!!" Greatly relieved, Ug and his men bowed to Bonga for the hospitality. Ug sent Pung back up the hill to get Pong.

Ug pointed to the hut that was obviously Bonga's and asked Kanush to apologize to the big man for destroying it. Kanush interpreted for Bonga and Bonga laughed again and said some words to Kanush. Kanush let Ug know that it was an understandable mistake and that Bonga owned several other huts in the village. He also had insurance. The hut makers had guaranteed that if for any reason the hut did not stand, they would rebuild it.

CHAPTER TEN
THE LAND OF OB

The Land of Ob was a large sprawling place with lots of vegetation and animals. There was a village square and huts that ran in a row for as far as Ug and his men could see. This was by far the largest village the men had ever seen. Once inside the village, Ug asked Kanush what these strange animals were that roamed freely in Ob.

Kanush replied, "The first we call baahaahaa. That's the one with the thick coat of hair. The next is called moooooo." The animals were named after the sounds that they make.

Erf asked Kanush if the animals tasted good. Kanush explained that the animals were not for eating.

"Not for eating?" questioned Erf with a look of indignant surprise. "What are they for?"

According to Kanush, the animals used to be eaten until the villagers from Ob found yet another great benefit. "Baahaahaa grows a thick coat of hair which is sheared with a sharp stone and made into coats that villagers wear during colder times. Moooooo makes a white liquid substance which can be drank warm or cold, which they call milk."

"Why do you call this liquid milk?" Ug wanted to know

"You see," started Kanush, "the young mooooooos would lick the older mooooooos on their underside and this white liquid would flow into the mouths of the young. So we used to call this liquid mooooo lick, like mooooolick. We shortened the word one time to moolick, then moolk, and finally decided on the word milk."

Bonga shouted to some men who quickly cleared a

---

section of the village square. Others brought a table and still others appeared with bowls of fresh berries, milk, and gazelle meat. To the starving Pong's great relief, Bonga gestured for the hungry travelers to join him in a morning feast. The men ate heartily and Bonga repeatedly called for the portions to be refilled. When all the men were completely satiated, Bonga asked the travelers to explain their business. Pong and Pung ran back to the village outskirts and picked up some of the wheels for the demonstration.

Pong and Pung returned, each rolling a wheel in front of them. Bonga said something to Kanush. Kanush turned to Ug and asked what these strange objects were.

"We call these wheels," Ug responded.

Ug started his demonstration and presentation of the wheel's use for Bonga, but the leader waved him off. He understood what the wheels were for. Bonga called for ten men to line up in triangular form in the middle of the village square. Ug and his men looked on in confusion. Bonga stood up, grabbed the wheel from Pong, and proceeded with a big heave to roll the wheel at the ten men. The men all screamed and tried to jump out of the way. The lead man escaped but the next two men fell backward, knocking down the remaining seven men behind them. Pong looked on with a smile of approval, but worried that his great new game invention had just been stolen. Bonga roared with laughter. He explained something to Kanush who interpreted for Ug.

"He likes the new game you've shown him. He thinks this will be a tremendous source of entertainment," explained Kanush. He would like to trade for the wheels.

Ug shook his head with disapproval. He explained to Kanush that the wheel was not invented for a game and, although this new game looked fun, it was dangerous. There was a much more important purpose for the wheel. Ug decided it was best to show the use of the wheel. He motioned for Mug and Mup to retrieve the cart that rolled into and knocked down Bonga's hut.

The men returned with the cart and Ug demonstrated how the wheel attached to the axles to make a cart that could transport goods. Kanush interpreted periodically for Bonga and the other Ob villagers.

Bonga shook his head in disagreement. He stubbornly had his ten men line up again in a triangle, shouting something loudly, and rolled the wheel towards the men. This time he knocked down seven of them. "Bonga says that is the best use for the wheel," Kanush explained.

Ug became visibly upset. He spoke rapidly, explaining how the cart could be used to transport items such as twigs for building and meat from the hunt. This was especially important with such a large village as Ob. Kanush again interpreted for Bonga. Bonga asked in his native language for Kanush's interpretation of how the cart was pulled. Ug ordered Mup and Mug to grab the vines connected to the cart and pull it around the village square. Bonga watched and shook his head again. He whistled for other villagers and they ran off between some huts.

"What is he doing?" Ug asked Kanush.

"You'll see," Kanush said.

THE WORLD'S
FIRST SALESMAN

Bonga's men returned with a moooooo. Wrapped around the moooooo's upper torso was a dead gazelle. Bonga explained and Kanush again interpreted for Ug. "You see, your cart and wheels require men to pull it and that is too much labor. We use the mooooooos to transport items so our men can save their strength."

Ug understood. With the help of his men, he grabbed the gazelle from the back of the moooooo and placed it inside the cart. He showed Kanush, Bonga, and the other gathered villagers that the cart could hold many more than one gazelle and, therefore, would be more efficient.

Bonga again nodded in disapproval, as did all of the other Ob villagers. "Too much work for men to pull the cart. We're afraid we have to reject this idea."

Ug was now extremely disappointed. He looked to each of his men for help. Mug looked away. Mup scratched his head. Pung looked at the ground. Erf raised his hands up in the air showing that he had no idea how to proceed. Gork looked up at the sky. Ug was feeling the terrible pain of rejection. They had come all this way. Maybe they hadn't greeted properly, but they had managed to establish rapport anyway. They had a revolutionary invention and because the village was large and on flat ground it was certainly qualified. But still these villagers from Ob were not interested.

Just then young Pong remembered the genius of Rap from the Village of No. He walked over to the moooooo and guided the large beast towards the cart. Pong positioned the beast in front of the cart, facing forward, with the moooooo's butt end facing the cart. The others, including

THE LAND OF OB

Bonga, Kanush, and the rest of the Ob villagers looked on in wonder. Pong stretched out the heavy vines that his companions has used to pull the carts. He wrapped the vines around the neck of the beast and tied them together. He gave the moooooo a swift pat on the butt and the moooooo began to move forward, pulling the cart with it.

Noting the look on Bonga's face, Kanush leaned in towards Ug and said, "Looks like the big man approves!" With that, the villagers of the Valley of the Sun were able to seal the deal.

The deal was sweet. Ug and his men would leave behind one of the carts and all of the wheels, and, in trade, they would take home three moooooos, five baahaahaas, and two cartloads of berries, gazelle, and milk. Kanush warned that they should return home quickly and drink the milk or it would spoil. Ug could not believe their incredible luck. Once again, he felt on top of the world. It was all due to the genius of young Pong. Pong had been the key to overcoming all rejection in the Land of Ob.

The men thanked their hospitable hosts and made their way home. On the way, Ug strategized some of his next moves. "Wow," he thought. "Young Pong really came through for the team." In order to build a worldwide, thriving enterprise Ug knew he needed a hot, young, up-and-coming talent in the executive ranks. His decision was made. Upon their return to the Valley of the Sun, Ug would promote Pong to the position of Vice President of Marketing and Product Development.

Halfway home the men stopped to rest and feast on

some of their hard earned goodies. Ug ate until he was full. He sat by the fire and reflected upon what he was beginning to believe was his larger mission, developing a system or a procedure to get his goods or any goods from the hands of the few, who invented and produced them, into the hands of the many, for whom those goods were useful.

He thought about how lucky he and his men were—thanks to the quick wit of young Pong—to have completely overcome Bonga's rejections. They were rejected first because they couldn't come up with the Proper Greeting and Establish Rapport with the sentries. But Pong's decision to roll the wheels down the hill and knock down so many villagers broke the ice and sent their chief into deep belly laughs that gave them a second chance for rapport-building. But even as they built that rapport with the help of Kanush, Bonga gave them rejection after rejection until Pong finally turned around the rejection by tying the cart to the large beast.

"Wow," thought Ug. We really overcame the rejection at Ob. Ug had learned something. Perhaps it was time to coin a new phrase for this next step in the process. Overcoming rejection at Ob. Overcoming Ob's rejections. Overcoming Ob-rejections, overcoming Ob-jections, overcoming OBJECTIONS!!!! He had it. And, with that, Ug fell into a peaceful and dreamy sleep.

The next morning when Ug and his men arose, Ug was considering whether they should attempt to make the third call of their journey to the Village of Nah. He asked his men and they all made a sour face, "Nah!"

CHAPTER ELEVEN

THE BIRTH OF
HUMAN
RESOURCES

CHAPTER ELEVEN

THE BIRTH OF HUMAN RESOURCES

U g and his men arrived home mid-day and shared much of their booty with the other village inhabitants. With all the villagers eating, drinking, and listening to the glorious stories of conquest from Ug and his men, it was like a large cave block party that lasted well into the evening.

The next morning Ug arose at the crack of dawn. He couldn't wait to visit the production line and determine how the new wheel manufacturing was coming along. To Ug's surprise, there were dozens upon dozens of wheels stocked up and waiting for new owners to take possession of them. "So many new wheels," Ug thought. "How will we move all of these? What if I don't sell this many? I still have to pay the workers for their time."

And thus, a new problem surfaced: Overstock. Ug felt a pang in his gut. "What have I done?" he worried. The men he had hired to assemble wheels no longer hunted for food. Instead, they were waiting for Ug to pay them with his newly acquired booty. Food stocks were running low and the days were becoming shorter. Hunting would be more difficult and soon it would be impossible. Ug knew that if the villagers went hungry, it would be his fault. He needed a way to get more wheels into the hands of more villages and bring a lot more food and drink back to the Valley of the Sun.

It was time to consult his executives about the situation. He had them all gather around the village tree so he could explain the situation. He asked the men for their advice. His key advisors now included Erf and Mug, his Junior Partners; Pung, Production Supervisor; and Pong, the new VP of Marketing and Product Development. Predictably, Erf and Mug just shrugged. Pung suggested they stop production for now and concentrate on the hunt. Ug agreed with Pung, but then young Pong offered a different idea.

Pong suggested they expand their sales operations. Currently, Ug was the only one really doing the selling. Pong believed that more villagers should go out and sell the wheels. If enough men from the village could be recruited to go sell, more wheels could be traded for more food. The villagers could survive this way, instead of going back to the hard days of hunting for food.

THE BIRTH OF HUMAN RESOURCES

Ug realized that Pong was making a valuable point. More folks on the road selling more wheels faster meant more booty for the villagers and better chances for survival. Ug asked Pong how he would go about getting more villagers on board to go sell wheels.

Pong suggested that they hire a gatherer. Only instead of gathering twigs and leaves for a fire or wood to make wheels and carts, this gatherer would gather villagers that wanted a new career.

"Interesting idea," thought Ug. A gatherer of resources. A gatherer of people, of humans who want to sell. Resources, humans. A gatherer of HUMAN RE-SOURCES. Ug knew it was the right solution. He immediately promoted Gork to be the recruiter, the gatherer, the world's first Director of Human Resources and the first sales recruiter.

Once the position was explained to Gork, he posed an interesting and challenging question. He explained that it was easy enough to show villagers how to knock down trees and make wheels and axles, but how were they supposed to show the new men how to sell? Ug scratched his head. Even Pong was somewhat befuddled with this one. How do they show men how to sell?

After a few minutes Erf suggested that they send the men out with cartloads of wheels and just have them wing it, hoping they might get some business. Pong and Ug weren't keen on that idea. The meeting went long and without a resolution.

Later that evening Ug decided to consult the wisest

man he knew. He headed over to Al's cave. Ug explained his current problem that they needed to recruit more men for selling wheels but didn't know how to go about training them for the task.

Al expressed a look of deep consternation while he pondered the problem. As the worry gave way to confidence and resolve, Al asked Ug to explain what he had learned in each village he had visited. Ug related each lesson and the concept he coined as a result of those lessons. At the Village of Grump, no one would do business with them because they insulted the Grump villagers with a bad greeting and so learned it was important to Properly Greet others. Next, in the Village of No, Ug discovered that you had to make friends with potential buyers, and the concept of Rapport was born. But even with a Proper Greeting and strong Rapport, they had found that you might have to go through many Noes to get a yes!!!"

"Good so far," said Al, encouraging the younger man to continue.

In Quali they learned that your buyer needed to be able to specify a use before they would acquire the product, so in essence you had to Qualify the buyer. Then, Ug told Al of the beautiful flock of birds flying in formation and how it had made Ug realize that part of qualifying the buyer was to specify their needs or expectations for them and educate them on how the product solved those needs or met those expectations. The orderliness of the birds made Ug realize that he could wrap those needs and expectations up like a present and give them to the potential buyer in the

---

form of a Presentation. But the most rewarding lesson of all, explained Ug, was the overcoming of rejections at Ob or, as he later conceptualized it, Overcoming Objections.

"That was it," explained Ug, still confused as to how all this could solve his problem. "We were going to see another village, but we had left all the remaining inventory when we filled the order at Ob so we came back for more."

"Brilliant," said Al. "There you have it. Your training program!"

"Huh?" said Ug.

"You see," Al began, "You have already discovered a simple process. First, you learned you have to Properly Greet others. Then you make friends or Build Rapport. Next, you must make sure the customer has a need or, as you put it, you must Qualify the Buyer. From there, you make a proper Presentation that helps them see their need for the product, and then you Overcome any Objections and Get the Order!!! You do all of this knowing that you may have to go through a lot of Noes to get a yes!!! Brilliant Ug!!!! There's your training program!!!"

Ug's jaw dropped nearly to the floor. The old man was right. The answer, easy: Properly Greet, Build Rapport, Qualify, Present, Overcome Objections, and Get the Order.

"Hmm… Get the Order," Ug's mind was churning again. He remembered that once they got the order from Ob, they were out of inventory and essentially closed for business until they restocked. Once they got the order, they were closed. Yes, the goal of each order should be that they are so large they essentially take all of the inventory so that

THE WORLD'S
FIRST SALESMAN

Ug's company is closed for business until they restock. He pondered this for a minute. "Make each order so large," he mumbled, "they take all of the inventory, and close us down until we get more stock. Order, close, Close!! And with that, Ug coined a new phrase for getting the order: The Close. Perhaps his training program really was complete.

Ug thanked Al profusely and headed back to his own cave where he would cuddle with his beautiful wife Lu whom he'd seen very little of for many weeks now and then get a good night's sleep. He was so excited he couldn't wait to get to work in the morning and tell his team about the new sales training program they would implement.

The next morning Ug awoke from a very peaceful and invigorating night's sleep. When he got to the business, he was the first one there. He realized that some day someone would invent a timepiece so others could know what time they had to show up for work. But that was in the future. For now, he would focus on manufacturing wheels.

The first to appear on the site was Gork, the new head of HR. Ug briefed Gork. Gork loved the idea and immediately set out towards the residential section of the village to knock on caves and recruit new sales trainees. Next, Mug and Erf showed up with Pung and Pong close behind them. Ug waited until they were all in attendance and briefed them on his training method. All four men were elated. Then, to Ug's amazement, Krat showed up and asked for his job back.

"You'll have to discuss the matter with Human Resources," Ug informed him. He reminded Krat of his

CHAPTER ELEVEN
THE BIRTH OF HUMAN RESOURCES

---

previous warning that, if he quit, he would not be eligible for rehire. Ug explained how he was now building a dream team of top village executives, salespeople, and laborers and had no time for quitters.

Krat began to cry. He told Ug he was sorry for letting him down and that he really needed the job in order to support his family. He explained how there were not enough men left in the village to go hunting because so many of them were now working for Ug.

Ug knew that he had better make things happen fast or the village would starve. He felt responsible for his old friend's condition and so agreed to let him back. However, he assured Krat for the final time that, if he quit, he would never again be eligible for hire at the International Wheel and Axle Company.

Krat thanked Ug for another chance and asked Ug if he could be an executive like his friends Pung, Erf, and Mug. Ug told Krat he'd have to start at the bottom and work his way up. Ug looked around and saw many loose piles of wood chips and other refuse around the company. He hired Krat as the janitor and told him he could start there and work his way up. Krat agreed and promised that no matter what, he'd never again quit.

For the first time in quite awhile, Ug decided to hang around the production line of the International Wheel and Axle Company and see for himself how things were going with the assembly line. Ug felt a great sense of accomplishment at seeing things working first hand. He watched the choppers chop down large trees, the cutters cut round

---

disks destined to become wheels, the shapers smooth each disk into an actual wheel, and the laborers move and stack the finished inventory. Ug looked at the growing stockpile of wheels and axles and did some quick calculations. The value was staggering. It added up to an equivalent of several cartloads of wine, berries, milk, and meat. If he could only move all of this inventory, his village would not only eat well through the winter, but every day would be a feast.

Late in the day Gork returned with four young men eager to become salesmen. Gork introduced the first two as Fup, son of Wup, and Krug, Ug's own nephew and son of Mug. But the two most promising candidates were Zig and Zag, the grandsons of the elder Al. Ug took the time to interview the young men personally. Each wanted the position and was eager to show their passion for the new career. Ug decided to hire all four of them, but this created a new dilemma: How to pay them? Ug decided to go home, eat some dinner with Lu and the kids and ponder this new challenge before he went to sleep.

After dinner Ug reclined against a rock in front of his cave. When Lu came out to check on him, she saw immediately that he was worried about something. Ug explained the problem to Lu. She sat down next to her man and pondered the problem with him.

"What happens if the men don't sell anything?" asked Lu.

"If there are no sales or not enough sales then there would not be enough booty to pay the workers and keep the operation going. We'd be forced to shut down and many

THE BIRTH OF HUMAN RESOURCES

villagers would go hungry."

"I certainly hope it doesn't come to that," she said. "But as far as paying your new salespeople, the answer is simple. If they don't sell, they don't eat."

Ug agreed that this was a good solution to his problem. Then he asked Lu, "What if they sell so much that they become the richest men in the village? What if they make even more than Ug?"

"That's a good thing," Lu responded, smiling. "I'd rather they be wealthy and sell a lot than be poor and not sell enough."

Ug agreed. "But what do I call this new pay system?" Ug asked his wife.

"I don't know," Lu said, not sharing Ug's inexhaustible need for new terms. "Come to bed, I miss you."

The next morning Ug met with Gork to discuss pay plans for the new salesmen. Gork agreed that a pay system for completed sales was the best way to compensate the new sales people. It would ensure that the salesmen were hungry and that they would do their job. Ug asked Gork for help in naming the new pay system.

Gork said, "Let's see... It's pay for completing a mission."

Ug began to play with the words, "Completed mission, complete mission, completemission, comp mission, COMMISSION! Ok, that works." And the world's first commission sales jobs were initiated.

Ug had four rocks placed about ten feet from each

other in corners to make a perfect square. On one side of the rock formation was a smooth pile of dirt and a stick. This is where Ug would lecture and draw diagrams in the dirt. Here, Ug would train his new salesmen. The first official training class of the International Wheel and Axle Company was about to begin.

The four eager young men, Fup, Krug, Zig, and Zag, all arrived ready to learn about sales. Ug called the class to order and congratulated the young men on being the first enrollees in a sales training program with the IWAC. Ug decided that a motivational speech was required to get these men in the learning frame of mind.

Ug explained to the men that this was likely to be the first of many training classes to come as the International Wheel and Axle Company continued to grow and become an inter-village economic force throughout the globe. Ug told the men of how this great invention had come about. Then he explained the concept for the axle and how it was needed to hold the wheels together. Next, Ug explained why he believed these new inventions would revolutionize the world. He spoke with deep conviction and watched as each of the four young men could hardly contain their excitement and eagerness to take action—to get out and sell.

"Most important to your success," Ug cautioned, "is learning the process of how to sell." He told them the story of how he and his men were chased away from the Village of Grump and how it was Al, the village wise man, who had pointed out that Ug misunderstood the greeting at Grump. "You must make a Proper Greeting to the prospect,"

CHAPTER ELEVEN
THE BIRTH OF HUMAN RESOURCES

---

explained Ug. "Otherwise you will not get any further in the process of selling."

Ug then explained how he discovered each of the next steps such as Establishing Rapport, Qualifying, Presentation, Overcoming Objections, and Closing. "This is the process, the way, the way to sell. Without it you will not be successful. With this process, the world is yours to conquer."

He watched as the young men nodded in agreement. But he wasn't satisfied. Explaining the process wasn't enough. The men needed to practice this concept. They needed to commit each step to memory, and, to be truly great, they needed to master each step by itself.

Ug decided the best way to train his new salespeople was to do some role playing. He cast Zig and Zag as the salespeople and Fup and Krug as the customers. He broke them off into two groups. Ug said, "Zig, you go this way. Zag, you go that way." And he had them practice and practice and practice each step until the sun fell and the workday was over.

By the next morning, Ug felt that his new sales crew was ready for the challenge. He decided to send them on the road in teams of two, with two additional men for each team to help with the carts and loads of wheels. He put Zig in charge of one team and Zag in charge of the other. He would send them on parallel destinations, close to each other so that Zig and Zag could occasionally cross paths and share notes. He also wanted them reasonably close to each other in case one group received an order that was too large to fill and the other had additional inventory.

Just before embarking on their destination, Ug had the men gather around the Village Tree. Also gathered were all of the workers and executives of the International Wheel and Axle Company and many of the villagers from the Valley of the Sun. Ug gave another pep talk to the men and explained that the survival and well being of the company and the village may very well rest on the shoulders of these four salesmen. The men confidently nodded at their new boss, accepting the challenge. As the men set off on their journey, their co-workers and the villagers lined up and cheered them on their way.

CHAPTER TWELVE

THE REBIRTH OF KRAT

CHAPTER TWELVE

THE REBIRTH OF KRAT

After the departure of the new salesmen, Ug spent his time wandering around the production line, watching workers, and having some casual meetings and discussions with his executives. Pong had come up with a new marketing slogan, "Four Wheels in Every Cave." Gork explained to Ug that he had a few more recruits that could be trained, and Pung briefed Ug on a production slowdown that was being handled. All seemed to be going well on the home front. Nevertheless, Ug was anxious about the endeavors of his new salesmen and the fate of his village. He wished there was a way to communicate with them to see how they were doing. He knew that one day someone would invent a way to talk to someone through a communications device even if they were very far away. He wondered if he would live long enough to see it.

Ug felt a tap on his shoulder. He turned to see Krat with a big grin on his face and covered from head to toe with dirt and sweat. Ug had forgotten about his old friend but realized then that the work site had never been so clean and efficient as it was with Krat as janitor.

"I want to be a salesman," Krat told him. "I pro- mise to make great sales and make you proud. And, I swear, I will never give up until I succeed."

"What do you know about sales?" Ug asked.

"I listened to you teach the others while I was clean- ing. I know I can do it. I know about Greeting, Rapport, Qualifying, Presentation, Overcoming Objections, and Closing. I want a chance. The village needs sales and I can do this," Krat swore.

Ug was dumbstruck. What a change in his old friend. Was this sincere, or would Krat just quit again like he had twice before. Ug needed to think about it so he informed Krat that he was satisfied for now with Krat's janitorial work and he wanted Krat to remain in that posi- tion and continue to prove himself. Clearly disappointed but with no chance of quitting, Krat agreed to continue as the janitor for a while longer.

Fourteen moons had passed and the days were be- coming noticeably shorter. The apprehension was sinking deeper inside of Ug. He was worried—worried that his salesmen would not succeed, or worse, that something bad happened to them in their travels. The men were gone longer than Ug had ever spent on any of his trips. The village food supply was dwindling fast. Wheel production was way down

THE REBIRTH OF KRAT

as many of the village men took time off from IWAC to go on an emergency hunt. The only redeeming factor was that this time the hunters took several carts, which were manufactured and donated by the IWAC. They would be able to return with more game than usual. But even that thought did not put Ug's mind at ease.

Ug called an executive committee meeting with Gork, Mug, Erf, Pung, Pong, and Al, who had been hired as a senior consultant to the group. He confessed his fears, which were shared by all the men. Ug had recently completed another training class for salesmen, but, at the last minute, had to let the men go on the emergency hunt.

"What shall we do?" Ug asked his top executives. None seemed to have an answer for him. Just then, Ug saw Krat furiously working to keep the workplace clean. He realized that for two weeks Krat had done exactly as he promised. Perhaps…?

"Maybe a last resort," Ug mumbled to himself. Ug's next thought was that he, Ug, should go back out into the field and make sales. He explained this plan to the others.

"Not a good idea," explained Al. "There's already fear and concern in the village that the company might not make it. There's worry about massive layoffs. I think if you, the Chief Executive, were to leave now, the villagers and workers would panic. This will worsen the situation."

Ug realized that he should take Al's advice because he was paying Al quite a bit.

Krat, who had been sweeping closer and closer to the men, was eavesdropping. He approached the group. He

THE WORLD'S
FIRST SALESMAN

---

threw down his broom and stood in front of the men. "You all know me, I am Krat, son of Brat, grandson of Gnat. I am a great friend to Ug, the world's greatest inventor.

"In the past I have let down my friends and fellow workers. I was a quitter. I did not see the wisdom in the wheel and the vision of the company. But I have changed. The wheel is one of the greatest inventions in the world. It will change the world in so many ways and make it easier for villagers everywhere to do their work, do their hunting, and to survive. Without the wheel, man is like any other beast. With it, man is king. The wheel opens a whole new realm of technological developments that will one day revolutionize the world into a thriving global community. However, the wheel is not the greatest invention.

The men all gasped. "Not the greatest invention? What do you mean?" Pong asked Krat.

Krat continued his sermon. "The discovery and invention of the wheel are profound and extremely important. Even more so because they have led to the greatest, most important discovery of our era. I have witnessed the training sessions for the new salesmen and studied Ug's new process for selling and conclude that this is the most important discovery of our time.

"Men were born to create things, but without the means and systems to sell them we have no way of sharing what we create, building on what others have created, and progressing as a species. Without sales, we are destined to continually reinvent the wheel… so to speak. Man was meant to interact with one another, village by village, valley by valley, mountain by mountain. How will we do that? By selling things. Through sales, we can create a global economy. Through sales, poor villagers like us can become men of great wealth and power. Through sales, one man, such as myself, could one day move out of his one room cave into a sprawling five bedroom cave with a pool and hot spa. Through sales, every villager can have not one, but two carts and a separate cave for the carts—a garage... a two-cart garage!!!

"You see," Krat went on, "Men have been trading things for some time now but never before on the scale that we now can with the invention of the wheel. In order for this new global economy to take hold, it was necessary for a great genius such as Ug to invent the process of sales, so it can be taught to others. Now that Ug has figured this out, the whole world will change. We can pass down this great technology, the technology of selling, from one generation to another until one day many will aspire to become sales-men—even women! Even women will want to sell and we'll call everyone salespeople."

The others laughed at what was clearly a preposter-ous idea, and they kept laughing even harder and louder to cover up what each felt must be the obvious truth that their wives would actually be much better salespeople than they ever would.

Krat was unphased by the laughter, but knew it was time to bring his speech to a dramatic close. "And so thank

THE WORLD'S
FIRST SALESMAN

---

you, distinguished gentlemen, for allowing me your audience. I, Krat, was born to sell. I know it now with every fiber of my being. I am here, put on this planet to be the great disciple of Ug, the world's first salesman. I therefore resign as janitor and wish to apply for the position of salesperson!"

Ug was totally speechless. This oration from Krat was almost unworldly. With such conviction and such desire burning within his friend, how could Ug deny him the opportunity to perform what Krat believed was his destiny. With a little reluctance but much hope, Ug bestowed the title of salesperson on Krat. The others applauded and with that, Krat was given a mission to complete—sell all the remaining wheels currently in inventory.

Ug suggested that Krat receive some more training, but Krat recited the sales process step by step and explained in detail what needed to occur in each step. Krat let Ug know that he had been practicing on his own and was fully prepared to meet this challenge.

Part of Ug's reluctance in sending Krat out to sell was that there were no other able-bodied men to assist him. But once again, Pong had the solution. Krat would go it alone with three cartloads of wheels and axles, and each cart would be pulled by one of the three moooooos the men had brought back from the Land of Ob. They immediately set about milking the moooooos before attaching each one to a cart. There was nothing left to do except say goodbye to Krat. Yet, it was with much anxiety that Ug and the others turned loose their old friend Krat to sink or swim as a salesman on the road by himself. Krat proudly accepted the challenge, went home to kiss his wife and kids, and was on his way.

CHAPTER THIRTEEN

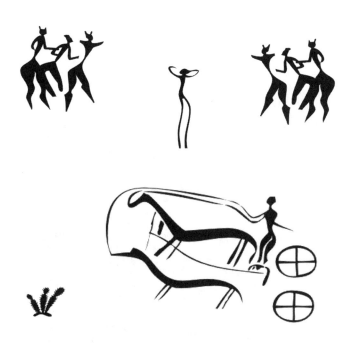

PERSISTENCE

CHAPTER THIRTEEN

PERSISTENCE

The village was in crisis. Fourteen more moons had passed with no sign of Zig, Zag, Fup, and Krug. Ug feared the worse. So did the other IWAC executives, but no one spoke about it. The emergency hunt yielded a scant amount of food for the villagers and many villagers had a hungry look in their eyes. Several that Ug had considered friends now looked upon him with disdain as though his pie-in-the-sky dreams of grandeur were responsible for the horrible condition the villagers were now in.

While walking through the village one Sunday morning, Ug was confronted with the fears and anger of many villagers.

"My children are hungry and it's all your fault!" one woman yelled. "If man was meant to have the wheel then God would've grown them on trees!" another villager sneered.

"We can't eat the wheels, you selfish idiot!" another

young villager screamed.

Ug continued walking and held his head up high, suppressing his tears. The tears of failure. "Perhaps I was too ambitious," Ug said to himself. "Perhaps I needed to think more about the needs of others than my own silly little dreams." Ug was a broken man. He told himself he'd give it all up as soon as the men returned safe from their journeys. Just then, he heard cheers from the far end of the village. Heart lifted in hope, Ug climbed a neighbors cave in order to see what the commotion was. Off in the distance, he could make out carts and four men approaching. Ug knew that it was Zig, Zag, Fup, and Krug.

Ug felt a surge of joy in his heart, but it was fleeting as the cheers were gradually replaced with boos. Ug strained to see what the booing was about and, to his horror, saw that the carts were nearly empty. The many cartloads of wheels were gone and there was just a small quantity of booty in each cart. He jumped down from his rocky perch and ran towards the men to get a closer look. When he was upon them, he could see that it was even worse than he thought. All of their carts were empty except one, which had a small amount of gazelle meat in it, only enough to feed the villagers for a few days.

The crowd grew even angrier as Ug approached. They even started to boo him. One small boy threw a rock that hit Ug on the leg. An elderly man spit at him. The crowd started to consolidate into a mob. Ug thought they might tear him limb from limb. Just then, Mug, Pung, Pong, and Gork surrounded Ug in a protective human shield. They all had sticks in their hands in case they needed to fend off the angry mob.

Al entered the scene and, with a voice of reason, convinced the mob to stand down. He then gestured for Ug, Mug, Pung, Pong, Gork, and the salesmen to follow him back to his cave for a debriefing.

At Al's cave, an angry Ug addressed his four salesmen, "What happened? You had several cartloads of good wheels and axles. They are now gone and in their place all you have is a few slabs of gazelle meat. Now the village may starve and it's all your fault!"

Al put his hand on Ug's shoulder, encouraging him to calm down and allow the men to speak their case.

Zig began, "We went to several villages and had mild success, selling a few wheels here and there, as samples mostly. Many villagers said if they worked well they would get more. We had a good amount of loot for our sales. Then we crossed paths and decided to go together to the Village of Rob. When we got there we did a fantastic Presentation, but the village leaders pretended they weren't interested and asked us to be on our way. We tried to Overcome Objections, but they wouldn't tell us what their objections were. They grew restless and it seemed they would be violent. So we left."

Zag took over, "Shortly after we left, a group of armed villagers approached us. They forced us to unload and hand over our remaining wheels and all of our loot. I'm sure these were men from Rob."

"But, then, how did you come to have any loot upon your return?" Ug asked in a much more humble tone.

Zig said, "We needed to eat so, on our way home, we did some hunting and got lucky enough to kill a little extra. We decided to bring it for the villagers."

Ug and the other executives felt the men were telling the truth. His salesmen, and now his village, had fallen victim to the awful people of Rob. From that moment forward, when someone took what didn't belong to them, the villagers referred to it as being "robbed." Never again would they call on the "Robbers" from Rob.

Although there was a fair explanation for why the men returned with no inventory and very little booty, the villagers were devastated. Ug was now sure he was through, and some of the villagers were calling for his head to be served on a platter.

"Well, men, I think it's over. I think you should turn me over to the villagers to suffer my fate," Ug informed his executives. "This endeavor has turned out to be a great failure, and I must shut it down and suffer the consequences."

As the other men nodded in agreement, Al stood up and cleared his throat for their attention. "Ug," Al said sternly, "You are a great inventor and a great leader. Krat was right. Your discoveries are some of the most important new developments known to man. Quitting is not the right thing to do. Persist. Continue with your plans. The wheel is important. Selling is important. One day these things will change the world. What you've learned from this experience is to plan better. That's all! No great accomplishment has ever been undertaken on this planet without having to overcome some obstacles and learn from mistakes. In this case, these obstacles are great, but so is the endeavor. You've come too far to give up now. The only way to achieve success is through persistence. In fact, if at first you don't succeed, try, try again!"

Al's words were uplifting to Ug and his men. But Ug knew that they still faced hungry villagers who feared for themselves and their children. Not enough food had been stocked from the hunt. The days were growing shorter and the frost was lasting longer each morning. It was a matter of just a few weeks that the cold season would be fully upon them and hunting would be impossible. Regardless of Al's wisdom, Ug knew something needed to happen soon or the village would be doomed.

Ug returned to his cave and curled up with Lu, hoping her loving embrace could help make his fears and worries go away. As Ug drifted off to sleep, he dreamt that his ancestors were smiling at him and encouraging him. He saw the face of his father and mother looking down on him when he was a little baby, and he heard the voice of his father telling his mother that one day their son would grow to be a great and important man. Ug smiled in his sleep, but then the dream changed. Light turned to dark. The friendly faces of family transformed into dozens of gaunt, hungry, and angry faces of the villagers. They had sticks and stones and were shouting at Ug. Ug tried to run. In his dream his feet moved rapidly, but he didn't go anywhere. The villagers were gaining on him. Some of them had fire shooting out of their eyes. He heard the shouts of, "Die, Ug! Die!"

As the villagers closed in on him with sticks poised to drive through his heart, Ug abruptly awoke. Lu held him tightly. "You fell asleep, my love. You had a nightmare."

"The situation is a nightmare, Lu. I let the village down and now many might starve because of my ideas."

"Nonsense," Lu responded. "You're a great man, Ug. It will all work out in the end."

Just then they heard some shouting from the edge of the village and it sounded an awful lot like happy cheers, and this time the cheers did not change to boos. In fact, the cheers grew into an outright roar of joy. Lu and Ug bolted out of their cave to see what all the commotion was about.

At the far end of the village, a large group had gathered, making it difficult to see what was causing the uproar. Ug and Lu jogged towards them. When they got to the crowd, Lu stayed behind while Ug fought his way through to the front. Coming toward them was a man followed by three heaping carts of loot, each pulled by a moooooo. About twenty men trailed behind the carts, some pulling additional cartloads of booty while others carried large gazelles on their shoulders. It was Krat. He'd come through! Ug could hardly believe it. His old friend had really come through.

Krat approached the crowd. He was rewarded with the loudest cheers ever heard throughout the Valley of the Sun. He walked within a few dozen feet of the crowd and stopped to let the mooooos loose to rest. The trailing men

---

all stopped behind him. Krat approached the crowd. He walked directly to his friend Ug and embraced him. Krat then lifted Ug in the air and the cheers grew even louder.

Krat quieted them and said, "This is my great friend Ug. The greatest inventor in the world. He is an important man and a true friend to villagers everywhere. Thanks to Ug and his great invention, I bring you the greatest booty the Valley of the Sun has ever received!"

"Now I must say," Krat continued, "although the wheel is a worldly and fabulous invention, were it not for Ug's greatest invention—the process of sales—I would not be here today ready to present this great bounty of sustenance for the village."

The villagers cheered loudly and several approached Ug. But this time without malice, sticks, or stones. A few of the stronger male villagers grabbed hold of Ug and hoisted him up on their shoulders and paraded him around the village. Women who were previously ready to throw rocks, now threw flowers. Men grabbed Ug's hands and thanked him.

One even said, "Thanks to Ug and his great wheel we can eat heartily for the whole season."

And so, that was that. Ug was once again rightfully recognized as the hero and innovator that he truly was.

When the cheering died down and the villagers returned to their own caves, Ug, Mug, Erf, Pung, and Pong asked Krat to join them in the center of the village under the shade of the large tree. Ug asked Krat how he came upon such bounty and who the men were that had followed him

---

back to the Valley of the Sun.

Krat explained in great detail how he had managed to close the greatest sale thus far in the history of the International Wheel and Axle Company. "You see," Krat began, "I came upon the Village of No where I was led by a few men to see a few more men and then even more and even more again until I met Rap. Rap said he was a friend of yours, Ug. I told Rap that you were also a friend of mine. He embraced me and said 'Port,' which I guess means friend in his language. Then he showed me in gestures that any friend of Ug's is a friend of his.

"He told me about how his village acquired the first wheels from you and how they were working out. He had a young boy bring in one of the wheels, and it was broken. He asked if I could fix it. I didn't know what to do. So I told him I would replace it at no charge. I told him that the International Wheel and Axle Company always stands behind its products. He was so thankful that, not only did he buy all of the remaining inventory I had, he also placed a future order for five-dozen more wheels. I told Rap of the situation in our village and how we needed food. Rap was very understanding. He sent many of his men with me. The extra booty they brought is a partial advance payment for the additional wheels."

Ug was overwhelmed. He felt like the luckiest man in the universe. He knew the wheel was important. But had it not been for the process of selling, none of this would have occurred. He asked Krat if Rap said anything else to him.

"Yes," Krat said. "He wondered why we waited so long to come back. He was nervous about what would happen if more wheels broke, but, more importantly, he wanted to give us a bigger order. He didn't know how to get in touch with us, and he asked that we follow up with him more often."

And just then a light went on inside of Ug's head. "Yes, yes, yes- that's it!" Ug exclaimed.

The other men looked at him with bewilderment.

"That's it. That's it!"

"What's it?" Krat asked.

"The next step in the process. Follow-up! How could we know if the customer is really happy and how can we get more business if we don't follow up!!! That's it! We must always follow up after the sale. That way we can fix any problems and ensure the customer is happy. Surely that will get the customer to buy more. Genius. Why didn't I think of that?"

"You just did!" Krat exclaimed, and all of the men, including Ug, laughed.

CHAPTER FOURTEEN

THE COMPLETE CYCLE

THE COMPLETE CYCLE

With some of the booty from Krat's sale, they had a grand feast prepared for all of the villagers and their honored guests from the Village of No. The feast was the first ever, official banquet sponsored by the International Wheel and Axle Company. Every villager attended and all had a grand time. The feast went well into the night and there was dancing and singing and great cheer. Everyone's spirits were at their very highest.

Ug personally greeted each man from the Village of No and thanked them for coming. The men felt special to be in the company of the world's greatest inventor. Ug ended the celebration with a speech thanking Krat for his persistence and success, the villagers for their support, and the men from the Village of No for their help and friendship.

THE WORLD'S
FIRST SALESMAN

The next morning, Ug consulted with his production supervisor, Pung, as to the amount of inventory on hand. It was determined that about half of the additional order for the Village of No could be filled. So Ug had his men load the carts that the Noes brought with them, and he sent one of his own carts as a gift to his friend Rap. Ug identified a tall strapping young man named Relay as the leader of the group from No. He told Relay to give a message to Rap. Ug's message was one of thanks and went like this:

> My Dear Rap,
> You are a good friend, indeed. Thank you so much for your order, for your friendship, and for lending your men for this important journey. Hope all is well. Please accept this new cart as my thank you gift.
> Your Great Friend,
> Ug

With that message and the loud and appreciative cheers from the villagers of the Valley of the Sun, the men from No smiled and waved as they made their exit.

Many happy days passed for Ug, his family, and the villagers from the Valley of the Sun. Wheel production was back at full throttle and the company was hiring several positions including accounting and IT. Back then, Information Technology consisted of keeping notches on trees to record workers' hours, production requirements, and other important data. The men even began discussing the possibilities of opening branch offices in other villages or licensing the technology so others could build the wheels. The days grew shorter and colder, but the spirits of the villagers grew brighter and stronger.

One day, about sixteen moons after Krat's return, Relay from the Village of No showed up in the Valley of the Sun. He had a message for Ug from Rap. The message was as follows:

My Dear Friend Ug,

You and your men have done such an outstanding job of servicing the needs of my village with your great wheels. So much so that I believe other villagers would benefit from the service and products that we received. Therefore, I am sending you the names of two great friends of mine that also are the heads of their villages. Their names are Ref, from the land of Prosp, and Eral, from the Village of Ect. Please provide them with your wheels and the same great service you have given to us. I will notify them that you will have someone visit them.

Thank you again.

Your Friend Always,
Rap

Ug was elated and decided to return a thank you message to Rap. He dictated it to Relay who would memorize it and give it to Rap. The message was as follows:

My Dear Rap,

Thank you so much for your kind words. I will indeed

take great care of Ref and Eral.

> Your Pal,
>
> Ug

Relay memorized the message. Ug asked him before he left what his main job was at the Village of No, and Relay responded, "To give and receive messages." Ug nodded and thanked the young man.

To ensure long-term memory, Ug repeated the names and places over and over. "Ref and Eral, from Prosp and Ect. Ref and Eral from Prosp and Ect. Ref Eral, Prosp Ect." Interesting sound, Ug thought. "Ref Eral, Prosp Ect." Ug almost made it into a song as he headed towards Krat to relay the information about Krat's next sales calls. "Ref Eral Prosp Ect."

Krat shook Ug's hand and asked how he was. Ug's response was, "Ref Eral, Prosp Ect."

Krat looked at Ug and said, "Huh?"

"I want you to see two new possible customers," Ug said. "Their names are Ref and Eral from Prosp and Ect."

"OK," Krat responded excitedly. "I'll go to Al's and get a map. On my way!"

"Ref Eral Prosp Ect," mumbled Ug. "A new addition to the process of selling. Oh, why not?" he thought. And Ug settled on the new term to describe possible customers who were recommended by others: REFERAL PROSPECTS.

Ug had every confidence in the world that his great new and persistent salesman would get the orders. Ug

CHAPTER FOURTEEN
THE COMPLETE CYCLE

decided to take the rest of the day off and go for a walk through nature. He walked among the trees at the outskirts of the village and reflected on how fortunate he had become. Not only would his wheel invention help revolutionize the planet, but so too would his process of sales. And finally, he knew he had the whole process down. He iterated it to himself:

- ° First - you must Properly Greet others.
- ° Next - you must Establish Rapport.
- ° Then - you have to Properly Qualify.
- ° With qualified prospects - you must make a good Presentation.
- ° Once presented - you have to Overcome any Objections.
- ° With all objections handled - you can Close.
- ° But closing the sale is not enough - you must Follow Up and ensure the customer is happy!
- ° If you have done everything right and followed up and the customer is happy - then they will send you Referrals!

"And," said Ug, "With that, you can start the process all over again with a new prospect. WOW!" The revelation hit Ug like a lightening bolt from heaven. "My Gosh" he thought, "This process of selling is just like the wheel—it's like one revolution of a wheel. Once you complete the process, you start all over again!!! It's like a wheel going round and round, never ending, just starting again at the beginning. Oh my, Krat was right! The greatest invention I've made is this process of selling—like one revolution of the wheel, one cycling through… That's it. The cycle—the Sales Cycle!! This cycle will truly change the world!!"

And, with that, you could say that in Ug's mind, THE WHEELS WERE TURNING!!!

CHAPTER FIFTEEN

JOHNNY'S NEW LIFE

JOHNNY'S NEW LIFE

Johnny beamed at Chance and said, "That was fascinating. I never really understood the basic path to selling until now. The sales cycle. Wow! I got it! I really got it."

Chance smiled. He checked his watch. It was nearly one o'clock in the morning. Years ago his father had made him promise to pass this story along when he found a bright young salesperson eager for the lesson. Chance felt content that he had fulfilled his promise with such an enthusiastic young man.

Johnny asked the waitress for a piece of paper. He slowly wrote down every step of the sales cycle, carefully describing what had to be accomplished at each. He looked up, "Chance," he started, "You truly are a good man and a good role model. I will never forget this lesson or you for as long as I live. There's a little Ug inside me now, and I think I can really turn around my sales career and be successful.

Thanks to you and Ug!"

Chance gave Johnny a genuine smile. "Johnny, I'm glad you'll take this lesson to heart. It's an important one. Now you know most of what I can tell you about what it takes to be successful in sales. Just one more thing: Always treat your prospects like your best friends and they will indeed become them."

"Just like you're treating me. You know, one day I'll be really successful and guess what?"

"What?"

"I'm going to get a million dollar life insurance policy from you!" They both laughed. But they both believed it.

Chance asked for the check. Johnny grabbed for it but before he could, Chance pushed his hand away and paid the check himself. "But...." Johnny began.

Chance waived him off. "No. No. I'm buying. After all, you're my prospect now."

They both laughed again. Chance paid the check and they walked out of the diner into the crisp night air. The diner wasn't far from where they had initially collided, and Johnny decided he wanted to walk to his car so he could look up at the stars and dream about his future.

Chance shook Johnny's hand and stuck a business card in his pocket. "You ever need anything, Johnny, just call. I mean it."

Johnny hugged Chance and thanked him again for a momentous evening. They went their separate ways.

Ten Years Later...

Chance's cell phone rings and he answers it. "Hello,

this is Chance."

"Chance old buddy, how are you?"

"Johnny?"

"The one and only."

"Johnny, how are Laura and the kids?"

"They're great, pal. Hey listen. I've got to tell you something."

"What's that?"

Johnny began, "The company just promoted me to Senior Vice President of Sales!"

Chance could hardly contain himself. "Johnny, that's awesome. You're only thirty-one! That's fantastic!"

"That's right. Youngest Senior VP in the history of the company and you know what?"

"What?" Chance asked.

"I owe a lot of my success to you!"

"Don't thank me—thank Ug!" Chance responded.

"How about I say I owe a lot to both of you," Johnny replied.

"That sounds good," agreed Chance.

"So I need to ask a favor of you, Chance."

"Anything Johnny, go ahead."

"I have a national sales conference that I'm heading up for over two hundred sales reps. This year's theme is 'Back to Basics in Sales.' I was wondering if I could tell them the story of Ug and his Revolutionary Invention?"

"That's a great idea Johnny. Your job, young grasshopper, is to take this great knowledge you now have and pass it along."

"Great, Chance. I thought you'd agree! Now about that life insurance policy, well with my income as a Senior VP and with Laura and the kids— well, forget the million-dollar policy—Let's make it two million..."

THE END

About the Author

Mr. Stuart Rosenbaum was born April 9, 1960 in Philadelphia, Pennsylvania. At the age of eighteen, shortly after graduating high school, he took a summer trip to Northern California, the area known as Silicon Valley. It was then that he knew that some day, he was going to move to this part of the country and become a successful businessman.

At the time, he had no idea of how he was going to accomplish this goal, however, while growing up, there were people in his life that kept telling him that he would be great in sales. At the age of twenty two, Mr. Rosenbaum took a position with a California firm owned and operated by his cousin Lee Ackrich. Lee was an exceptional sales person and thus Mr. Rosenbaum was able to learn a good deal from him. Among his other mentors was Lee's wife Provy, who was also a professional sales person, top producer and sales manager. Provy was the one that handed him his first book on sales, Og Mandino's "The Greatest Salesman in the World." From there he began to understand that selling was more than just the ability to talk to people, in fact Mr. Rosenbaum learned that the selling profession was one filled with passion in order to truly become successful.

As part of his personal quest to become a stellar sales person, he learned many of the basics from great trainers and motivators such as Tom Hopkins and Zig Ziglar. He took his sales career seriously and studied to be great at it, once he realized that the selling profession is truly that- a profession.

By the age of thirty five, Mr. Rosenbaum had started seven different companies, three of which were successfully built and sold, and the largest, US Merchant Systems, which he still runs today in his capacity as CEO. Furthermore, he had held board seats on four different companies, and one association, the American Home Business Association.

Although he is mostly considered an entrepreneur and businessman, Mr. Rosenbaum likes more to consider himself as a professional salesman. His greatest aspiration, however, has always been to be a writer. Throughout his professional career he had written many articles, ads, training materials and sales scripts, which helped to develop many successful sales representatives through out the United States.

In 1992 Mr. Rosenbaum co-founded US Merchant Systems. Since then, the company has grown from three employees to sixty corporate employees and hundreds of independent sales agents. Since inception the company has provided its services to more than 100,000 businesses. Mr. Rosenbaum has spoken at electronic transaction industry functions, and has been featured in articles for publications that include the SF Business Times, The Green Sheet, Transaction Trends Magazine, Small Business Magazine, The Advantage Networker and others. He has been interviewed on radio programs including CEO Cast and is a highly respected member of the Transaction Industry and member of the Electronic Transaction Association.

QUICK ORDER FORM

Fax orders: 510-687-2108. Send this form.
Email orders: sebastian@usms.com
Phone orders: 1-800-655-8767 x 2108
On line orders: Www.SellingWarriors.com
Postal orders: Selling Warriors Publishing Co. 1115 Delmas Ave. # 3. San Jose, CA 95125-1722, USA.

Please send the following books. I understand that I may return any of them in perfect conditions for a full refund-for any reason, no questions asked.

_____

_____

Please send more FREE information on:
Other Books____
Speaking/Seminars____
Consulting____

Name:_____
Address:_____
City:_____State:____Zip:_____
Telephone:_____
Email address:_____

Sales Tax: Please add 8.25% for products shipped to California addresses.

Shipping and handling withing U.S.: $ 4.00 for one book.
Flat rates avalaible for quantity.

QUICK ORDER FORM

Fax orders: 510-687-2108. Send this form.
Email orders: sebastian@usms.com
Phone orders: 1-800-655-8767 x 2108
On line orders: Www.SellingWarriors.com
Postal orders: Selling Warriors Publishing Co. 1115 Delmas Ave. # 3. San Jose, CA 95125-1722, USA.

Please send the following books. I understand that I may return any of them in perfect conditions for a full refund-for any reason, no questions asked.

_____

_____

Please send more FREE information on:
Other Books____
Speaking/Seminars____
Consulting____

Name:_____
Address:_____
City:_____State:____Zip:_____
Telephone:_____
Email address:_____

Sales Tax: Please add 8.25% for products shipped to California addresses.

Shipping and handling withing U.S.: $ 4.00 for one book. Flat rates avalaible for quantity.

SELLING WARRIOR
PUBLISHING CO.